HER LAST HOPE

JEN TALTY

Jupiter Press

"Deadly Secrets is the best of romance and suspense in one hot read!" *NYT Bestselling Author Jennifer Probst*

"A charming setting and a steamy couple heat up the pages in an suspenseful story I couldn't put down!" *NY Times and USA today Bestselling Author Donna Grant*

"Jen Talty's books will grab your attention and pull you into a world of relatable characters, strong personalities, humor, and believable storylines. You'll laugh, you'll cry, and you'll rush to get the next book she releases!" Natalie Ann USA Today Bestselling Author

"I positively loved *In Two Weeks*, and highly recommend it. The writing is wonderful, the story is fantastic, and the characters will keep you coming back for more. I can't wait to get my hands on future installments of the NYS Troopers series." *Long and Short Reviews*

"*In Two Weeks* hooks the reader from page one. This is a fast paced story where the development of the romance grabs you emotionally and the suspense keeps you sitting on the edge of your chair. Great characters, great writing, and a believable plot that can be a warning to all of us." *Desiree Holt, USA Today Bestseller*

"*Dark Water* delivers an engaging portrait of wounded hearts as the memorable characters take you on a healing journey of love. A mysterious death brings danger and intrigue into the drama, while sultry passions brew into a believable plot that melts the reader's heart. Jen Talty pens an entertaining romance that grips the heart as the colorful and dangerous story unfolds into a chilling ending." *Night Owl Reviews*

"This is not the typical love story, nor is it the typical mystery. The characters are well rounded and interesting." *You Gotta Read Reviews*

"*Murder in Paradise Bay* is a fast-paced romantic thriller with plenty of twists and turns to keep you guessing until the end. You won't want to miss this one..." *USA Today bestselling author Janice Maynard*

HER LAST HOPE

AN AEGIS NETWORK NOVELLA

the SARICH BROTHERS series
book 2 of 5

Nick's Story

JEN TALTY

ACKNOWLEDGMENTS

A HUGE thank you to my nephew-in-law, Nick
Chorley, for letting me borrow his name and taking me
out for the best pulled pork ever and driving me
around Windermere, telling me all about the history of
the area, which gave me the idea for this story! Thanks,
Nick!

And I have to thank my niece, Shea Holbrook, for
letting me stay at her home (which I use in this story)
and driving me all around Lake Butler, also telling me
stories, and laughing at my questions and ideas. Oh,
and we can't forget making me grab Superman's junk!
LOL. However, it is Batman who makes an appearance
(had to change the name to protect the innocent).

I also mention in the book that the owners of the house
are racecar drivers. Well, Shea is a racecar driver. To

learn more about Shea, check out Shea Racing (shearacing.com). She's one cool, badass woman!

The Aegis Network is the brainchild of former Marines, Bain Asher and Decker Griggs. While serving their country, Bain and Decker were injured in a raid in an undisclosed area during an unsanctioned mission. Instead of twiddling their thumbs while on medical leave, they focused their frustration at being sidelined toward their pet project: a sophisticated Quantum Communication Network Satellite. When the devastating news came that neither man would be placed on active duty ever again, they sold their technology to the United States government and landed on a heaping pot of gold and funded their passion.

Saving lives.

The Aegis Network is an elite group of men and women, mostly ex-military, descending from all branches. They may have left the armed forces, but the armed forces didn't leave them. There's no limit to the type of missions they'll take, from kidnapping, protection detail, infiltrating enemy lines, and everything in between; no job is too big or too small when lives are at stake.

As Marines, they vowed no man left behind.
As civilians, they will risk all to ensure the safety of their clients.

Some researchers have said there is a correlation between the ocean and being calm, happier, and more creative. Having spent a winter in Jupiter, Florida, I'd say these researchers are right on the money.

The SARICH BROTHERS series was born while I spent four months in Jupiter, walking the beach, visiting the Jupiter Lighthouse, driving around Jupiter Island, dining at various places on the water, and overall enjoying this next chapter in my life known as the 'empty nest.'

The Sarich brothers, while poor, had a good life, raised by loving parents. However, their father was killed in the line of duty when the oldest boy was just twenty and the youngest fourteen, changing their lives forever...

Each of the brothers struggle with a restlessness, in part caused by their father's death. They are strong, honorable, and loyal men. They aren't looking for a woman, as their jobs aren't necessarily conducive with long-term relationships. It's going to take an equally strong woman to rip down the Sarich brothers' defenses and help them settle their restlessness, so they can give their hearts.

The series does not need to be read in order, but the four novellas do follow a timeline.

Come join each of the Sarich boys in their journey to heal old wounds, mend broken hearts, and find their way to true happiness with the love of a good, strong woman.

I want to add that since this series has been released, and then re-released, my readers have begged me to write Mrs. Sarich's story...well, it's coming! Look for Catherine's story, THE MATRIARCH, on January 12, 2020.

Sign up for Jen's Newsletter
(https://dl.bookfunnel.com/rg8mx9lchy) *where she often gives away free books before publication.*

Join Jen's private Facebook group (https://www.facebook. com/groups/191706547909047/) where she posts exclusive excerpts and discuss all things murder and love!

For my Family

---

*T*he clear night sky, filled with stars, cast a white glow across the water. A warm summer breeze rippled the dark-blue lake as the thick scent of dead fish lingered in the dense air. Nick Sarich put the zodiac boat in neutral and cut the engine in front of a two-million-dollar home on Lake Butler, in Windermere, Florida. A quaint little town outside of Orlando that attracted everyone from your average Joe to the rich and famous.

Not to mention a few criminals.

Darkness had been a good friend to Nick, both in the field and in his heart. Everyone told him that, in time, he'd be able to get past the loss of his wife and unborn child. Even his mother told him that someday he'd want to live his life again. He'd bitten his tongue every time he wanted to remind his mother that she'd never moved on after his father had died. No boyfriends. No dating. Nothing but work and sitting around waiting for one of her four sons to settle down and have a bunch of little Sarich grandbabies.

However, if he dared speak his mind, his mother would grab him by the ear, giving it a good tug, and that generally hurt. Not to mention, he did have the best mother any man could hope for. Disrespect was not in the Sarich' vocabulary, at least not the intentional kind.

He tossed over a fishing line as he scanned the front of the ten-thousand-square-foot home. A string of lights dangled around the fence separating the pool area from the lake. Lanterns glowed on the dock posts, illuminating a life-size statue of Batman. The dark knight's cap flapped with the breeze.

Every detail seared unwillingly into his brain. The experts called it a photographic memory.

He called it a curse.

But this evening, sitting in the dark, peering into the few open windows of Moises Ramos' home, watching Ramos and a few of his cronies smoke cigars and sip whiskey by the pool, his memory came in handy as he mentally pulled up the case file on Leandra Whitfield, his first official mission as a member of the Omega Team.

Bain Asher and Declan Griggs, the founders of the Aegis Network, had handed him this assignment right after his older brother's engagement party, and while Nick didn't begrudge the eldest Sarich, Logan, his happiness, he couldn't bring himself to be truly exultant for the ecstatic couple.

Not knowing that Logan's soon-to-be wife was also a soon-to-be mom.

He blinked the painful thoughts away, focusing on the picture in his head of Leandra from the file. Stunning woman. No. Dangerously sexy. Her long dark hair matched her wild, chocolate eyes. Her rosy lips offset her porcelain-like skin. He smiled at the image of her sitting on a Harley, sporting a white tank top and one badass tattoo on her right shoulder. It looked like some sort of infinity symbol with lettering, but the photograph was too small to make it out. She smiled in the picture, all sweet-like, but Nick saw one tough interior to match the woman on the bike. It screamed: don't mess with me, I bite.

Oh, how he wouldn't mind being bitten by a woman like Leandra.

Focus.

He mulled over the laundry list of information. She was a twenty-eight-year-old military widow, a pain he could understand, and from what he'd read, she'd done exactly as he had, tossed herself into her work. Smart girl.

She had her own private investigation firm located in Brooklyn, New York, her hometown. Her file said she'd moved back there from Jacksonville, North Carolina, two months after her husband had been killed, another decision he could relate to.

She'd recently been hired by a family to find their missing daughter, and then five days ago, Leandra went missing herself.

The fishing pole bobbed, and Nick snagged it from its holder and reeled in a not-so-impressive fish while eyeing the house. Thus far, he'd only seen the five men sitting outside along with four guards. Their laughter filled the night air like smoke in a closed chimney.

As he snagged the fish, preparing to take out the hook, a voluptuous woman stepped from the sliders.

The fish hook gripped the flesh on Nick's thumb.

"Fuck," he muttered, quickly sucking on his finger, staring at Leandra as she walked across the patio in what could only be described as fuck-me heels. Her wide hips swayed under the moon. Her toned legs flexed and captivated him from under her criminally short miniskirt. Nick let his eyes wander up the rest of her full-bodied figure, though full wasn't the right word for it. She just wasn't a bean pole. She was what women should aspire to look like, with her curves being in all the right places.

Nick tossed the fish back in the water, tossing his inappropriate thoughts with it, though the tightening in his groin hadn't eased up at all.

An exotic woman with dark skin and flowing dark hair followed Leandra outside. He'd seen the tall lady a few times and figured she was one of the many women that dressed Ramos' arm. Even Nick had to admit the man was attractive, but why any woman would want to be with someone who had a reputation like Ramos was beyond Nick.

He shook his head. Like he was any better just because his one-night stands knew that's all they were.

Leandra leaned against the fence, laughing with the men at some perverted comment that degraded women.

Nick drew his lips in a tight line.

What the hell was Leandra Wakefield doing with the likes of a drug-pushing, underground casino ring leader?

And what did that have to do with a missing girl?

Everything he'd learned about her thus far indicated she always immersed herself too far into her cases, and she'd gotten herself into difficult situations.

Often with the potential of death.

But he supposed that didn't matter anymore since he'd found her. He was hired to bring her back to daddy, so that was exactly what he intended to do.

Tonight.

He tossed the fishing line over as the boat drifted closer to shore. He knew the best way onto Ramos' property was through the waterfront. All he had to do was wait for them to go to bed and then find the room where Leandra rested her pretty little head. Hopefully, she wasn't crazy enough to sleep with Ramos in the name of solving a case.

He pushed that thought out of his head and focused on how much fun he'd have covering her mouth and carrying her out of the house as she fought him.

Kidnapping a woman shouldn't be a turn on, but when Leandra turned her head, looking out over the lake, her white skin being kissed by the moon, Nick knew he'd never enjoy anything more.

*L*eandra let Ramos kiss her cheek as he patted her ass, giving it a firm squeeze. She tried not to shiver in utter disgust. It didn't matter that the man's body looked like it jumped right out of a fire-fighters' calendar, with his dark skin, green eyes, and full lips that made most women swoon.

She wasn't most women, and Ramos was the armpit of the earth.

"I'm glad you took me up on my offer to be my guest." He looked her up and down, smacking his lips, his fingers still digging into her ass.

"I don't think your current girlfriend would appreciate you groping me right under her nose."

"Alicia isn't my girlfriend." Ramos licked his lips. "She works for me and couldn't care less who I fuck. Hell, she might even join us."

Leandra swallowed the bile that smacked the back of her throat. "This is a business arrangement. Nothing more." Whatever had made her think she'd be able to sneak around his house in the middle of the night while he slept, she had no idea. Security cameras lined all the corridors, and armed men roamed inside and out. Luckily, she'd done a comprehensive sweep of her room, and so far, she'd found no cameras or bugs.

Now she just had to fend off his advances a little while longer.

Or worse, fend off an attack.

He grabbed her hand with his slimy fingers and

brushed his lips against her skin, drawing her a little closer with the other hand. "I think we should make it more."

"I don't mix business with pleasure," she said in a stern tone, lowering her chin. With heels, she had him by three inches. Flat-footed, her five-foot-eleven-inch frame put her eye to eye with Ramos. It was possible he could overpower her.

But the reverse was also true.

"All right then. Is everything all set?" Ramos asked, his hand still on her butt-cheek. His breath reeked of whiskey. "Because I'd hate for you to disappoint me."

"I told you this isn't my first rodeo." Researching the human trafficking racket didn't make one an expert in the field, but neither was Ramos, since he'd only branched out from underground casinos and drug running in the last few months. "I also told you my contact doesn't like doing business with someone who is as secretive about their operation as you are." She inched away, peeling his hands off her body.

"I don't know *your* guy," Ramos practically snarled, narrowing his eyes. "Why should I trust him?"

"Because I trust him."

"I don't trust a woman who won't fuck me."

She forced a smile, tilting her head. "I'm married, so I'm not going to fuck you." Her stomach churned. Kent, her late husband, had supported her career decision as a private investigator, but he didn't like it when she took cases like this, and during their marriage, she never had.

Sorry, Kent. But it's the only way I can survive without you.

He arched his brow. "I don't care, and I bet I could make you forget all about your man."

"I'm not going to bed with you. Now we either move forward, or I'll walk out tonight, and you'll be stuck with merchandise you can't move."

The way he adjusted his pants, obviously shifting his package, giving it a good shake, made her body go cold. Her skin tensed as goosebumps prickled the surface.

"I wouldn't have to house them long. I'm sure I could find buyers quickly."

She forced a smile. "Except you've got a Fed up your ass, and your buyers are running scared, which is why you came looking for me."

"That's not how I remember it, sweetheart." He licked his sun-cracked lips. The deep-set lines on his overly tanned face looked more like scars than wrinkles. "As I recall, you took one man's unfounded paranoia and turned a profit for yourself." He winked. "I wouldn't be surprised if you made my buyer more paranoid just to get the business yourself."

She shrugged. "Wouldn't be the first time a woman went after what she wanted."

"That's such a turn on." He grabbed his junk and smiled. "Hmmmmmm. You're lucky I've got my fill of women right now, or I'd be bending you over right here."

She swallowed. "My husband wouldn't take too kindly to that, and frankly, neither would I." She forced a smile. "No offense, but we'll make better business partners."

"We shall see," he said, adjusting his belt. "If your guy doesn't show up by tomorrow, consider yourself mine in a different way."

"Ramos?" Alicia's voice called out from down the hallway. The clicking of her heels on the tile echoed off the walls. She smiled coolly as she approached. "We've got a little bit of a problem," she said, resting her hand on his shoulder.

"So handle it," he said with frustration laced in his tone. "That's what I pay you to do."

"I did handle it." Alicia smoothed her hand down his arm in a possessive manner. "But your manager at the Holding Tank doesn't like what I did and is now demanding to see you. He's sitting on the front porch. I told him you were busy."

"That man is such a pussy," Ramos said with a grunt. "I think it's time to put him in his place."

Leandra shivered. Those words could mean anything.

"I'll leave you to your business. Good night." She turned on her heels and headed down the long corridor, wondering if the Holding Tank was one of his casinos or something else. She paused, glancing over her shoulder. Ramos walked down the hallway with Alicia, his hand on her ass. Following them would be dangerous, and if he found her poking around, well, then this might go down as the worst situation she'd ever gotten herself into.

And bad situations seemed to follow her around.

The bedroom door clicked closed, but she knew better than to lock it. If Ramos found out, the circle of trust would be broken.

Not that he trusted her.

It didn't matter since she had no idea how she was going to pull 'a guy' out of her butt that could pretend to know a thing or two about the human trafficking market. Her father always warned her that bluffing would someday bite her in the ass that Ramos had just violated.

She kicked off her heels and flung herself on the bed. She really should sneak out tonight and never look back. If she left now, she could be back at her apartment in Brooklyn, New York, in two days. Of course, that would be forty-eight hours of looking over her shoulder.

The fan above her hummed as the blades whirled, sending warm air across her already heated body, but not it a good way. Why southerners thought eighty degrees on the AC as a set temperature was acceptable, she'd never know. She pushed herself to a sitting position and took her phone from the nightstand.

Not a single contact had gotten back to her. She swallowed the tickle of fear that rose from the pit of her stomach. She'd give her buddies until four in the morning. If no one came through, she'd have to make a run for it. A tear formed in the corner of her eye. She'd promised Mr. and Mrs. Denton that she'd find their daughter, Skyler, no matter what.

Leandra rubbed her eyes as she entered the bathroom and splashed cold water on her face. Staring at her reflection in the mirror, she heard faint footsteps. She peered out of the bathroom but saw nothing—unless you counted the guards just walking around the big house. She slipped from her clothes, opting for a more comfortable pair of shorts and a tank top. Not that she didn't like to dress up occasionally, but she'd take a pair of jeans and a T-shirt any day of the week over dressing like she belonged on the catwalk, especially being 'curvy' or 'a little round' as her size four mother called her. Mom thought she was being nice in her choice of words, but it stung just the same.

Being raised by a beauty queen who was born with a silver spoon in her mouth had been a challenge for the tough-as-nails tomboy, Leandra. She and her mother had struggled to get along their entire lives, but now things were tolerable as long as her mother didn't remind Leandra what men liked in a woman.

Leandra turned off the main light, keeping the small lamp next to the bed on. A shadow moved across the window. She shivered. Sneaking out wouldn't be that easy. She'd have to time things perfectly. There were only four guards on the property, but they were heavily armed. She sent messages to a couple of her private investigator friends, begging for help on this one. All she needed was to buy a little time.

She tapped her tablet and opened her document on

Ramos. He'd started out as a two-bit hustler, working his way up to running one of the biggest underground casino rings, and now he was running people.

Another shadow darted across the window opposite the wall. It was impossible to ignore that right down the hall was a stone-cold killer. She reached across the bed, pulling her weapon from her suitcase on the floor, cocking it, resting it next to her, and keeping her finger on the butt of the gun.

The rustling of something outside startled her once again. Her stomach tightened into a fist of knots. Scrolling on her tablet, she found the picture of Skyler Denton. Beautiful eighteen-year-old young woman with sandy-brown hair, cut to her shoulders in the front, much shorter in the back. Leandra ran her fingers across the screen, just under Skyler's ice-blue eyes. In the picture she smiled, arms looped around her brother and sister, her parents standing proudly behind them.

"I'm going to find you," she whispered just as she noticed a shadow in the bathroom. Grabbing her weapon, she scooted to the side of the bed, raising her arms and pointing the gun toward the door.

Paranoid.

And seeing things.

No one would climb through the window in the bathroom. At least no one from Ramos' organization.

Or would they?

On tiptoes, she eased across the room, pressing her back against the wall. The slight screech from what could have been a soft-soled shoe echoed from the bathroom. The noise could have also been leaves rustling against the window. She sucked in a quiet breath. It made no sense that one of Ramos' guys would come at her like this. They'd just barge through the bedroom door.

She let her breath out as she shimmied against the wall until her shoulder touched the molding of the door. Pivoting on her heels, she lunged through the door, weapon drawn. Her heart pounded so hard against her ribs she worried one would break.

Nothing.

She held her weapon steady as she scanned the small room, finding no one and nothing disturbed.

She shook her head, blinking. When she took on this case, she thought it was a simple missing person. A teenage girl who had run away from home, more than once, hooked on drugs and probably prostituting herself. Skyler had done all of the above the last time she'd run away. But this time? Leandra believed she'd been kidnapped.

Skyler had left her parents' home, ten months sober and on her way to a college class where she'd been getting straight A's. Her purse, backpack, and phone had been found in the parking lot of the community college.

Worse, none of her old friends from her days on the streets had heard from her, much less seen her.

Leandra turned toward the mirror and gasped as a tall, well-built man dressed in black lunged from the linen closet. She twisted, shifting her gun, but he managed to grab hold of her wrist with a firm grip. His other arm wrapped tightly around her body, hauling her back tight to his chest.

"Be quiet," he whispered. His blue eyes held her gaze in the mirror. His chiseled features sent a shiver down her spine. But it was the way the corner of his lips tipped upward that made her pause. She should think him menacing, but that smile made him look as if he were hitting on her from across a crowded bar.

With her free arm, she jabbed him in the gut with her elbow. He groaned, but his rock-hard stomach didn't flinch. As she prepared to nail him again, he yanked her arm down, smashing it against the counter, sending her weapon spinning across the top, knocking over the soap dispenser.

"Fuck," she muttered as he covered her mouth with his hand.

"Shhhhhh." He smiled at her in the mirror. "We don't want Ramos knowing I'm here."

She narrowed her eyes into tiny slits and dug her heel into his foot.

Grunting, he pushed her against the sink, bending her slightly at the waist, pinning her. "Stop fighting me," he whispered. "I don't want to have to hurt you."

Taking in a deep breath, she let her body relax a little into his while two things came to mind: How the fuck did he get in that linen closet with his size, and no way would she stop fighting.

"I was sent to help you."

By who? she wondered, because none of her contacts had gotten back to her, and they wouldn't send someone without warning. Her heart pounded. She told herself it was fear, but it wasn't, not completely. She laced her fingers around his powerful forearm, feeling his muscles flex against her touch. She tugged.

"I'll uncover your mouth if you agree to follow my directions explicitly."

She shook her head again. Following someone else's instructions had never been her strong suit.

He arched a brow.

Reaching up, she tried to pry his hand from her mouth. His long, thick fingers twisted, holding her hand as steady as his blue eyes held her in a captivating stare.

She should be trying to get away.

But she found herself wondering what it might be like to have this man kiss her lips, a thought she hadn't had since the first time she'd met her late husband. However, it gave her an idea.

She wiggled her ass against him in just the right spot, flirting as best she could with her seductive gaze. His eyes widened as the pressure increased against her butt. Then he smiled and pushed harder.

"You really want to play that game?"

The sexy man holding her tight pulled out a Smith and Wesson Magnum .500. Impressive weapon to match an impressive man. She swallowed.

"Are you going to be quiet?" he asked.

She let out a long breath and rolled her eyes. Not the smartest thing to do in a situation like this, but she'd been around enough bad guys to know this man was a badass, but not a criminal. The way he stood and held his gun gave away his military training, and she could spot a military man a mile away. Then again, there were some good military men who turned to the other side.

But the man in mirror? He held her firmly, but not with too much force. Even in this position, pinned to the counter, his touch was more gentle than hurtful.

Leandra had good instincts, and she trusted her gut. Whoever this man was, he wasn't there to cause her harm.

He cracked a smile as he slowly uncovered her mouth.

"Who the hell are you?" she whispered, trying to break free from his grasp. "And more importantly, who do you work for?" While her gut was almost never wrong, there was still a chance her captor worked for Ramos in some capacity.

"Who I am is irrelevant. Your father hired me to save you."

She narrowed her eyes. "First, I don't need saving." She wiggled, rotating her shoulders back and forth. He tightened his hold. "Second, I don't believe you work for my father because I don't have one." At least her alias didn't. "Tell Ramos this is the dumbest loyalty test ever. He keeps pulling this shit and my guy will run for the hills." She let her voice go from a faint whisper to a hush toned.

He covered her mouth again.

His eyes twitched and narrowed as she smiled behind his hand, letting her tongue touch his palm.

"Be careful, hon. I'm one of the good guys, but I'm not a saint." He pressed his lips against her cheek. His touch felt like a moist feather sticking to her skin.

"I know exactly who you are. You're Leandra Wakefield, private investigator out of Brooklyn. Daughter of multi-millionaire Chester Wakefield. Not Leandra Waters and whatever crazy bio you created for yourself." He continued to stare at her in the mirror, his gun pressed against her shoulder, his large arm wrapped tightly around her middle. His gaze never wavered, but his eyes glimmered, waking up the erogenous zones that had been asleep since her husband died.

Who got turned on by being held at gunpoint?

Maybe she did have a death wish.

She'd carefully crafted her aliases for jobs like this one, but unfortunately, she hadn't had much time to plan, and her assistant hadn't spent hours looking for holes in it.

Shaking her head, she managed to free her mouth from his grasp once again. "Tell Ramos that I've scheduled a meet for tomorrow." She squirmed, contemplating rearing her leg up between his and landing her heel right where it counts.

He must have read her mind as he cocked his head and repositioned himself. "We can do this the easy way or the hard way." He tapped the butt of his gun against the back of her head.

Her heart skipped a beat.

"Your father hired me to bring you back to him safe and sound, and that is what I intend to do. In eleven minutes, we have to be out that window and high-tailing it to the fence at the west side and down to the waterfront."

"I'm not going anywhere with you." She twisted herself, hard and quick. Leaning forward, she raised her foot, going right for the groin.

She missed.

He had the nerve to smile.

"Asshole," she muttered.

Grabbing his forearm, she pushed her ass against him, twisting his body, flinging herself backward. They hit the wall with loud smack. Raising her arm, she hurled her elbow into his gut. This time he hunched over, and she went for the gun.

"Oh, no, you don't." He shoved her forward, snagging both of her arms, yanking them behind her back. He pressed her body over the counter, this time holding her chest down. Her shoulders burned as he pulled harder on her wrists.

"This kind of noise is going to bring a shitstorm we don't need."

Lifting her face from the counter, she looked at him once again in the mirror. The jerk still had a stupid smile plastered across his face.

She grinned back, though she hadn't meant to.

Nor did she welcome being turned on.

"Keep this up and I will render you unconscious," he said.

"Let me go." She drew her lips in a tight line, forcing her mind to remember this man didn't want to woo her into bed.

"Not on your life, hon." He jerked her body upward and toward the window.

"I'm not your *hon*, and I'm not going anywhere with you." This time she lifted both feet off the floor, pressing her feet against the sink and giving them both a good shove. He stumbled backward, twisting his body away from the wall.

She kicked her legs, trying to lock her feet under the towel rack, but missed about the same time he regained his balance.

"Sorry, hon, I didn't want to have to do this, but you've left me no choice."

The world went into slow motion as he lowered his weapon toward her head. A loud crack echoed in her ears, followed by intense ringing. Black squiggly lines that looked like little maggots filled her vision. More and more of them covered her sight until the world went black…

2

*A*ll Nick could think about was how disappointed his mother would be that he'd just assaulted a lady. Sure, a badass lady, but a lady nonetheless.

And the widow of a Marine.

He pressed the bag of frozen vegetables against the already growing lump on the back of her head, scowling. Her body was sprawled on the sofa in a small house not far from Ramos' mansion. The house was owned by a young couple who raced cars and were currently out of town for the next month at various racetracks. The Aegis Network had secured the house for Nick's use for three weeks. Thus far, he'd spent three days there, following Ramos, studying the layout of the area, and working out an exit strategy for Leandra.

Now that he had her, he wasn't hell-bent on returning her to daddy dearest. No. He wanted to find out what this chick was up to and why she was hanging around a scumbag like Ramos.

Nick sat on the coffee table in front of the sofa, keeping the cold compress on her head, staring at her angelic face. He'd long gotten over the feeling like he was betraying his wife every time he had sex with a woman. It was just sex. He didn't mean that to sound crass, but relationships were out of the question.

He just wasn't capable.

Joanne had been the love of his life. The only woman for him, and he'd lost her and their child to a boating accident that could have been avoided had the other driver only been paying attention. The hardest part of that day had been holding his wife as she took her last breath, saying the words "I love you" and smiling when she did so.

He blinked. He needed to remind himself he'd never find that kind of love again, nor did he want the pain that went with it. His mother always told him he'd been one of the lucky ones, having found the kind of connection he'd had with Joanne. When she'd been alive, he had known it to be true. He'd been the luckiest man in the world. But now that she was gone?

He clutched his chest.

Love sucked, and no way would he ever allow himself to feel so deeply for another woman again, even if she made his heart beat a little faster and made his mind wander to places he'd shut down years ago.

Leandra groaned as she shifted on the sofa, reaching for the back of her head. He continued to press the cold bag to her head, even when she tried to bat him away.

Then her eyelids fluttered. A sweet, soft moan escaped her lips as she arched her back. As soon as he saw the dark-chocolate color of her eyes, she bolted to an upright position.

"What the fuck!?" she yelled. "Who the hell are you? You're ruining everything..." She winced, pushing his hand away and flinging the cold bag of vegetables across the room. "I need to get back before they know I'm missing," she said, her voice fading off as she rubbed the back of her head.

"What are you doing with the likes of Ramos? Are you working for him?" Nick didn't believe she'd crossed the line, but he needed a distraction from the feelings she stirred inside him.

Physically, she was perfect for him with her soft skin and round curves, not to mention her height. His six-foot-one-inch frame probably only had two inches on her, and that was a turn on all by itself. When he'd lifted her over his shoulder, the excitement of feeling her body against his consumed him. He told himself it had been too long without physical contact with a woman.

The rest of his thoughts he couldn't explain and didn't want to explore.

Besides, she was a widow of only two years. He was well past ten, and he still hadn't been able to consider anything but sex, and even that took much contemplation on his part.

"Yes and no." She maneuvered herself to a sitting position. "Now tell me who you are, besides military."

"What makes you think I'm military?"

"My husband's a Marine."

He frowned. He couldn't remember how long it had taken him to refer to his wife in the past tense.

"Was a Marine," she whispered.

He nodded, staring into her eyes, trying to suck in all her pain. She deserved the ability to move on with her life and live it to the fullest.

"I'm sorry for your loss." Standard response, but so was *thank you for your service.* However, he appreciated the words every time someone said them. "The name's Nick. I work for The Aegis Network—"

"The what network?" She rubbed the back of her head.

He winced as her face scrunched in pain. Hitting her hadn't been the highlight of the evening.

"A group of ex-military men and women hired for special jobs. This op is all about bringing you home to your father."

"I told you I don't have a father," she said as her gaze darted around the room. Her wide-eyed expression searched for a way out.

"Cut the bullshit, Leandra." He inched closer and cracked a slight smile when she didn't lean away. As a matter-of-fact, she puffed out her chest, holding her ground.

Feisty and strong.

And still in love with her dead husband.

Mentally, he laughed at his thought. He'd never stop loving Joanne.

"I know everything there is to know about you."

Her eyes widened and then narrowed into tiny little slits. "I doubt that."

"Your father gave me quite a lot of information. But I was also in your apartment a few days ago. I know you have a small table in the entryway where you have a seashell dish, which I assume you dump your keys in. Your kitchen isn't much, but it's obvious you like to cook by the expensive pots and pans you own. Not to mention you have a ton of cookbooks. I also know you only seem to have thong underwear. Your bra size is a 38D, your jeans are a size 12, and—"

"You're a fucking pervert." She stood, kicking the coffee table as she shoved it aside, standing over him with her hands on those goddamned voluptuous hips.

Seriously, the moment he had five minutes free, he'd have to find himself a one-night stand.

Slowly, he stood, exerting his powerful body over hers, only she wasn't someone most people would want to mess with. He rubbed his side where she'd nailed him twice, knowing a bruise had formed. "I'm no such thing, though I will admit to having a veracious appetite for sex, but searching your apartment was all part of doing my job."

"Checking out my panties isn't doing your job."

He smiled. "You just confirmed that you are indeed, Leandra Wakefield."

"Fine. You got me." She shifted her weight, her

breasts bouncing slightly. "Now you're going to say goodbye."

"Nope." He waved to the sofa, and thankfully she sat down. "I'm Nick Sarich." He shoved out his hand. "Nice to meet you."

"Not," she muttered, letting his hand hang in the air. "So, my father hired you because I didn't call him for a couple of weeks."

"No. He hired me because you never showed up for a blind date."

"Crap," she muttered. "I forgot about that. How the hell did he know where I was?"

"He didn't." Nick snagged the cold bag and sat down next to her as he pressed it against the lump he'd made on the back of her head. "I found you."

"Well, un-find me, because I've got a job to do, and my father knows I'm a big girl and can handle myself." She shrugged his hand away after taking the bag.

Had Nick been an ordinary man, she could have easily overpowered him in the bathroom, taking control of the situation, but Nick wasn't average.

Then again, neither was she.

"You've been missing for a week," he said. "Not a single phone call and when you missed your date, your father got worried."

"I'm sure my mother was more concerned about the fact I ditched a friend's son, but I have a job to do, and I intend to see it through," she said in a stern voice. One that he suspected made many a man quake in his shoes.

But not Nick.

No. She had an entirely different effect on him.

"What's the job?" He wanted to slap himself for asking, partly because he knew the basics of the case.

"I thought you knew everything about me?" She cocked her head, her full lips pursed together like a lipstick commercial where she was about to kiss something, leaving behind a lipstick impression.

All he could think about was kissing her mouth with enough force that it would make her lips swell. "I know you wax yourself." That was an asinine thing to say. He cringed, waiting to be smacked, but all she did was stare at him.

"Do you know if I wax it all off, or leave a little behind?" Her sarcasm wasn't lost on him, but her slight grin sent his mind tumbling to a place where he'd yank her pants to her ankles to find out.

"I'm guessing all of it. Or maybe hoping."

She turned, tucking one leg under her voluptuous ass. "And I bet you manscape, enjoying the hot wax on your body before ripping it off with exquisite pain."

He became fully aware that she wore nothing but her pajamas, and the thought of her being totally bare tightened his groin.

She leaned forward, pressing her arms against her sides, the movement bringing her breasts together and thrusting them further out of her top. "I bet you're the kind of man who likes to have his control stripped." Her moist breath tickled his skin as she kissed his neck.

The sofa shifted and before she could stand up and make a run for it, because he knew she was playing him, using her body...one he couldn't ignore...he snagged a fist full of her hair.

Her eyes went wide.

"Hon, I wouldn't play this game if I were you," he said.

"Who said I'm playing anything?" She smiled as she gently placed her hand on his thigh, dangerously close to his growing erection. "You've got me all hot and bothered." Her nervous smile showed a vulnerability he couldn't handle.

He blinked a few times, forcing himself to break the intense gaze. "As much as I'd like to flip you over on your back and toss your legs over my shoulders, I've got a job to do."

"Well, I've got news for you." Her fingers dug into his thigh muscle. "I'm not going back until this case is closed. You can tell my father you found me. Hell, I'll even call him. But I'm not leaving."

"Maybe I can help you with your case." With his hand still holding her hair, he tugged slightly, exposing the soft curve of her neck. He pressed his mouth on her skin, feeling her pulse beat against his lips. "And when we're done with that, I'll help you get that first fuck after your husband died out of the way."

She jerked her head back. "Excuse me?"

He glided his fingers through her thick, dark hair, before dropping his hand to the sofa. "You haven't had sex since he died, have you?"

"That's none of your fucking business, and it has nothing to do with you helping me with Ramos."

"Fair enough." He smiled. "But you're still leaning over me with your breasts close to my mouth and your hand..." He looked at his thigh.

"Point taken," she said, shifting to a sitting position, making sure not a single part of her body touched him. "Sorry."

"Don't sweat it." He rolled his head, staring at her profile. The light from the lamp hit her just right, showing off her porcelain-like skin. In all the years since Joanne had passed, not a single woman had turned him on the way Leandra did.

And it wasn't just physical.

"Staring at you in the mirror with my hand over your mouth, I had some interesting thoughts. Like bending—"

She jabbed him with her elbow. "No need to express it. You're a perv, and I've turned into a crazed, sex-starved widow."

"I'm not a pervert." He scowled. "And I've been where you are. Wish I could say it gets easier."

"Not at all?"

He shrugged. He couldn't remember the last time he'd told a woman he'd been married, much less that his heart had been so shattered, it barely pumped blood. "My wife died shortly after we were married. I vowed I'd never have sex again. Now that's all I do."

"All you do?"

He laughed. "I don't do relationships. But we've gone so far off the issue at hand. Tell me how I can help with Ramos and your case." He clasped his hands behind his head and stared at the ceiling.

She let out a long breath, resting her head on the back of the sofa. "Ramos is running a human trafficking ring."

"And how exactly does that affect you?"

"My client's daughter is one of seven young women missing in a twenty-five-mile radius over the course of a week."

"When was she abducted?" The tension between his legs had simmered down, but it hadn't fully gone away. He suspected it might never with her close by.

"About a month ago."

"She's probably long gone by now."

"I know, but if I can get into where he keeps them, I might be able to find his records and find to who and where she was sold."

"It's a long shot."

"But I have to take the chance. After doing some more digging, I've found a pattern in different locations in Florida regarding missing young adults." The passion fused in her voice sealed his fate.

He'd do whatever it took to help her.

Then fuck her.

"There are a lot of missing kids all over the country, and that doesn't make for a pattern of any kind," he said.

"It does when three victims in the last four months were found alive, all telling the same story."

"And what story is that?"

"A ring of human traffickers. Each kid was from a different area. One from Miami, one from the panhandle, and one from Ft. Myers." She locked gazes with him. Her deep-chocolate eyes danced with adrenaline, something he knew well. "The identical details each gave to the authorities about their abductors couldn't be coincidence."

"Do you have case files on these?"

She nodded.

"I want to see them."

"I don't need or want your help."

"Either I stay and help, or I take you to your father now." He didn't give her a chance to respond. "What do the cops say?"

"They're looking into the victims' stories, but all three had been runaways prior to this most recent disappearance and had been into drugs or prostituted themselves at one point. The cops don't think much about most of the missing kids since half of them had been or are troubled teens, and the other half, over the age of eighteen."

"So, they believe they were all runaways." Nick had spent a few years as a local police officer and knew the drill. Often, with missing kids over the age of sixteen, unless there had been substantial evidence that an abduction had occurred, an Amber Alert wasn't even issued. It was a catch-22 because many of these runaways got themselves in some deadly situations, but many didn't fit the criteria for an Amber Alert. "Which brings me to why you're staying in Ramos' house." He looked into her dark, succulent eyes. "You went from a hotel ten miles away to his house."

She arched a brow. "You've been watching me?"

He nodded. "I needed to figure out how to get in and out without getting us both killed, but it also appeared that you and he were..." Nick looked at the ceiling. "...friendly."

"That's downright disgusting," she said under a tight lip.

"I'm teasing you."

"I'm not laughing."

He nodded. "So how did you end up at Ramos' mansion?"

"I found out Ramos needed a quick sale since his regular buyers backed out. Not to mention he has to move the current group because of this Fed that's been poking around. I decided to give Ramos a solution by providing him with a new auctioneer with his own contacts."

"That doesn't explain why you're sleeping in Ramos' house." A thought that disturbed Nick on way too many levels.

"I rang his doorbell."

Nick coughed. "You're kidding, right?"

She shook her head. "I had approached him at a restaurant, and he blew me off, so I showed up, and he admired my big balls."

"I don't want him admiring anything about you," Nick said under his breath. "Was staying a condition of getting the gig?"

"Partially, but I didn't want him to check out my car rental, so I Ubered."

Smart, but not so smart.

"Where'd you find the buyer?"

"Haven't found him yet." She tossed the vegetable bag on the table. "But Ramos wants to meet my guy tomorrow and do the sale as soon as possible."

"Who's your backup, and how do you see this going down?"

"I have none, and I have no idea."

"What!? Are you fucking crazy? And this is all supposed to go down tomorrow?"

"I need to find my client's daughter, and this is the only way." She stood, leaping over the coffee table. "I need to get back. My phone and laptop are both there, and one of my contacts could be trying to reach me."

"You think I just fell off the turnip truck?" He pointed to the dining room. "I gathered all of your important things that I could find."

"I still need to get back before daybreak." She planted her hands on her sexy hips again.

Hips that he wouldn't mind grabbing in the heat of the moment.

Fuck. What the hell was his problem?

She made it worse by shifting, as if she knew his mind had just plummeted into the gutter.

"What time is this meeting tomorrow?" he asked.

"I told Ramos I'd have an exact time and place by morning." She rocked back and forth, shifting her weight from one leg to the other.

"But if you can't make that happen by tomorrow, you're as good as dead."

She let out a sarcastic chuckle. "After Ramos has his way with me, which I suspect he's beyond kinky or perverted, and I doubt I'd like it much either."

Nick balled his fists. The idea that Ramos might lay even his pinky finger on Leandra made his blood cells burst like exploding popcorn.

"Consider me Batman. I'll be the buyer, and I can get a team of men here in a few hours to do the rest." He stepped up the two stairs dividing the family room from the dining room. Grabbing her round hips, he turned her.

"What am I supposed to be? Cat Woman?" Her hands rested on his shoulders. "I doubt that is the right costume for me."

"Oh, hell yes," he said, giving her hips a squeeze. "You were made for that costume."

She tilted her head, giving him an inquisitive stare. "This isn't a good idea."

"No, it's not."

"For all I know you work for Ramos and you're setting me up."

He cocked his head as he slinked his hands to the small of her back. Bad idea was putting this situation mildly. "Call your daddy and find out who I am."

Her fists came down hard on his chest as she balled his shirt, heaving him forward. He counteracted, but found himself tumbling backward, holding her tight, taking her with him.

"Fuck," she mumbled, pulling back, but it was too late as he tripped backward over the steps, scrambling to make sure they made it to the sofa and didn't land on the floor, but clutching her tight, anticipating her landing on top of him, her round breasts smashed against his chest.

Maybe he was a pervert after all.

She dug her heels into the carpet, while her fists pulled at his shirt, slowing them down enough that when his ass hit the sofa, he slid to the ground with a thud.

A painful grunt echoed from her lips when her knees hit the floorboards.

A pleasurable groan escaped his throat as her body landed on his thighs, his fingers digging into the top part of her ass.

"That didn't go as planned," she muttered.

"I don't know about that." He winked. "I kind of like how it ended."

"Ugh. Let me go, or else—"

"Or else what?" For fuck's sake. He was acting more like his womanizing little brother, Ramey. And there was a difference between having a romp in the sack with a woman who gladly understood and accepted what he was looking for versus going through women, leaving a string of broken hearts along the way.

His broken heart had been enough.

Not to mention Leandra's.

She leaned over, her hot breath on his ear. Her fingers glided down his chest in an erotic dance that tossed him off-balance, sending a warm shiver across his skin.

He swallowed.

Her eyes turned a seductive dark brown with a hint of a sparkle as she raised up on her knees, her hand at the top of his pants.

"We need to stop this." Dropping his hands to his sides and his head to the sofa, he took in a few deep, calming breaths. He tried to snap his focus to the operation and not the sexy woman sitting on his lap. "I'm sorry. I've behaved incredibly inappropriately, and I have no excuse." He could tell Leandra that he'd been all fucked up since the day his wife had died and how things got compounded a few weeks ago when his older brother got engaged and then dropped the bomb that his bride-to-be was pregnant, but that would make him sound even crazier than being perverted.

He closed his eyes, waiting for her to stand up, but instead she plopped herself right back on his lap.

He groaned, unable to control his body's reaction to hers. "Keep sitting like that and I won't take responsibility for what happens next."

"I'm a big girl," she said in a faint whisper. "Who are you really, and why do you make me crazy?"

"I can't answer the second one." He dropped his forearm over his eyes. "But to the first one, I'm just an ex-Army guy hired to do a job, and I'm really good at what I do."

"Are you one of the good guys?" Her fingers laced

around his wrist, tugging, while her other hand tilted his head. "I need to see your eyes."

He blinked as he let all the air in his lungs swish out in a single pant. "When it comes to what side of the law I stand on, I'm a great guy."

"Good."

"Now please get up so we can devise a plan to bring down Ramos and find your client's daughter, or I will grab you again, because when it comes to bedding women, I'm not a man who sticks around, so in that department, I'm a bad guy."

Her mouth moved closer to his, and it took every ounce of control he had not to flip her on her back and strip her naked. When her lips brushed against his, he gripped the sofa cushion. Her beautiful eyes searched his with a combination of lust and confusion, matching his own swirling emotions. "I don't want a man to stick around."

"You're playing with fire," he whispered.

"I know."

He groaned, cupping her cheeks and shoving his tongue deep inside her mouth. She tasted like honey-suckle on a warm summer's evening. His body shivered as she sucked on his tongue, taking command of the kiss, torturing his mouth. Her fingers dug into his shoulders. Everything about this woman made him dizzy. Not only did he want to bury himself in every part of her body, he wanted to hold her in his arms, caress her soft skin. Kiss her temple and watch the stars together.

Yanking his lips from his, he stared into her eyes. "Save the girl first. Put Ramos behind bars. Then we fuck like there is no tomorrow."

"Sounds good to me."

A deep growl vibrated from his throat.

He'd just met his match.

3

*L*eandra wrapped the big white towel across her body before wiping the steam off the mirror. No matter how long she stood under the hot water, she couldn't get Nick's sexy touch off her body.

And honestly, she didn't want to.

But she had to.

The focus had to be on finding Skyler and the rest of the missing kids before they were sold into slavery all across the globe, never to be found. Though she knew Skyler had most likely been unloaded already, a thought that haunted her every waking moment.

She slipped on her thong, remembering how quickly Nick grew hard as she straddled him. When he'd grabbed her, an electric pulse shot through her body. The lust in his eyes commanded her body like a conductor controlling his orchestra.

And that kiss.

Wow.

She shook her head, running her fingers through her wet hair. Thoughts of screwing the man senseless needed to stop. It shocked her that she'd even thought about another man other than her husband that way. In the last year, her family had decided it was time for her to date. She'd put them off, but her mother wouldn't let it go and went about fixing her up with every single man she knew.

Some of them were hot, too, but she couldn't picture herself getting naked with them, much less wanting to take their manhood into her hands and mouth, or anywhere else for that matter.

Ugh.

She finished getting dressed before putting on her makeup, trying to hide the dark circles that had suddenly appeared under her eyes. She'd tried to get a couple of hours of sleep once Nick had helped her back through the bedroom window at Ramos' house, kissing her gently on the lips, telling her to be safe, and if at any point she wanted out, all she had to do was call him and he'd come rescue her.

The theme song from Batman raced through her mind.

Taking her phone, she made her way down the long corridor to the kitchen where the smell of rich coffee mingled with bacon and cinnamon, causing her stomach to growl.

Stay away from starch, especially in the morning, because it will set the tone of the day.

Her mother's words rattled in her brain. Leandra

knew her mother meant well, now. But when she'd been a freshman in high school and weighed in at one hundred and seventy pounds, the words sent her into full-out body shame, something that took the love of a good man to get rid of.

She rubbed her wedding ring finger. Taking her diamond off had been almost as hard as watching the Marine Corps Chaplain and her late husband's commanding officer walk up the short path from the street to her front door. She'd held the knob for what seemed like an eternity before she'd been able to pull it open, collapsing to the floor, sobbing.

"Good morning." Ramos leaned against the sliding glass door that overlooked the pool and faced the lake.

Alicia nodded from behind her computer screen. Leandra couldn't figure her out or what exactly she did for Ramos, but the woman seemed to always be around.

"Morning." Leandra smiled in her direction, but Alicia barely smiled back.

Leandra turned her attention to the stunning view of the lake. Five boats were anchored in the water not far from the house. Leandra wondered which ones were part of the team Nick had assembled. The resources that man had were astounding.

"Sleep well?" Ramos asked.

"I did, thank you."

"Did you hear from your man?"

Game on. "He wants to meet at eleven in the morning. Here." Ramos stood behind her, hands on her shoulders, rubbing. The sensation made her body stiff and cold. His touch felt like a snake coiling around her stomach, ready to squeeze the life out of her.

Alicia continued to stare at her computer screen, her fingers tapping away.

"I don't know about here." Ramos sat down and waved the cook over, who set a plate of French toast, bacon, eggs, hash browns, and a cup of coffee in front of her.

"You control the situation here over meeting somewhere else." She sipped her coffee, inhaling the bitter scent as the aroma of cinnamon tickled her nose. She'd always had a healthy appetite, and she'd been active, playing field hockey and other physical sports. The idea that a woman should be a twig had been a foreign concept to her, but society dictated the perfect body for women, and she didn't fit the mold.

"Thank you," she said politely to the cook before setting down her mug and cutting into the thick sourdough bread. Nothing like a hearty breakfast.

Fitting the mold was for those who wanted to blend in, not stand out.

"What's this man's name?"

"Nick," she said, knowing he was on the lake, looking in at her, watching her, protecting her.

An odd thought because she never thought she needed protecting.

Ramos leaned back in his chair, fingers scratching the small patch of hair on his chin. "And what are you getting out of this, because the finder's fee I'm paying you doesn't seem worth it."

"Nick and I are partners," she said, doing her best to be casual. Nick remembered everything, something she'd learned in her first hour with him last night. Her memory? It was good, but they hadn't spent much time developing this plan, which meant the margin for error was greater than she'd normally have.

"Are you fucking this man?" Ramos traced his finger up her thigh toward the hem of her skirt.

"He's my husband, so yeah, we fuck." She brushed Ramos' hand from her thigh. "And he wouldn't take too kindly to you hitting on his wife." She swallowed as the word 'wife' left her lips. That hadn't been part of her and Nick's carefully laid out plan, but she hoped Ramos, who valued loyalty more than anything, would now keep his greasy paws off her.

Alicia peered over the computer screen. "Sorry to interrupt, but I just wanted you to know it's done."

"Good." Ramos continued to dance his fingers across Leandra's skin. "I think you have a meeting, don't you?"

Alicia closed her laptop and stood. "I'll let you know the outcome."

Ramos nodded. He watched Alicia's hips sway as she slinked out of the kitchen.

Leandra swallowed the bile burning her throat.

"Alicia is sexy as hell, but she's a cold fish," Ramos whispered into Leandra's ear. "I don't like it when people lie to me." Ramos kept his slimy fingers on her leg. "And I don't care if your husband would be bothered by this." His fingers slid under her skirt. "Because I am going to fuck you."

She choked on a piece of bacon as she batted his hand away. After taking a slow sip of water, she wiped her mouth and turned to face Ramos. "I'm not a liar, so I can promise you, we will not be going to bed together."

He leaned back in his chair, clasping his thick fingers behind his head. The corners of his mouth tipped up in the kind of grin that made her skin prickle with fear.

"How does your husband feel about you staying here with me?"

She shrugged. "He trusts me, and he'd kill you if you laid a hand on me." She smiled, cocking her head. "But I'd kill you first."

"I like this side of you." Ramos adjusted himself.

She kept her gaze on his eyes, not the mound between his legs he tried to get her to notice.

"You're a sexy woman, and I bet you're a real tiger in bed. I suspect it takes a quite the man to satisfy you. I know you'd be happier with my dick inside you than your husband's."

Conjuring up the sensation of having Nick between her legs and the way his lips sizzled against hers, a huge smile spread across her face. "Highly unlikely."

He waved to the cook, raising his empty mug. "Text your husband, if that is who he is, and tell him the meet is on. I assume he knows I'll have eyes everywhere."

She nodded, nibbling on more bacon.

"Do it now."

The command startled her but didn't surprise her. She pulled out her phone and pulled up Nick's contact information, which had his last name as Manovich.

Hey, babe...meet is confirmed, Wifey.

She set the phone on the table, face up, so Ramos could view the text.

Transparency.

Pushing her plate aside, she glanced out the window, focusing on one of the smaller fishing boats. She couldn't see the man's face, but he held something in his hands and by his frame, she could tell it was Nick. He didn't glance up, but at the same time he stuffed something in his pocket, her phone dinged.

Perhaps we move it up? As planned?...Hubby XOXO.

"What does that mean?" Ramos shook his head, dropping his hand to the side.

"Means he's out there." She pointed to the lake front, then texted:

Your call...Wifey.

Ramos pushed back the chair, the legs screeching across the tile floor like fingernails on a chalkboard. "How dare you," he said with a snarl. "I generally kill people who spy on me."

"It's a public lake, and there are a dozen fishermen out there. Only one is my husband, so I wouldn't call it spying."

Ramos turned, grinning. The way he sauntered

toward her made the hair on the back of her neck stand up.

"You're a smart woman. Let's hope that husband of yours is as smart," Ramos said.

"He married me, didn't he?"

Ramos patted her shoulder as he glanced out at the lake. "If you manage to fuck this up, I'll kill your husband, but not until after he's watched me make you cum like no one else could." His smile turned her blood to ice. The food in her stomach churned.

"I don't take kindly to threats in the middle of a business deal." She kept her tone level as she curled her fingers around the coffee mug, doing her best to appear indifferent to his comment. A smile tugged at her lips when she saw Nick pull a small boat up to the dock, though she quickly frowned when three of Ramos' men pointed their weapons on Nick.

"I don't know if I should be disappointed he's stupid, or excited that I'm going to get to taste you." He ran his thick fingers in her hair, tugging until her face tilted upward, then forced her to a standing position. Out of the corner of her eye, she watched as Nick stepped forward, only to have the men raise their weapons, inching closer.

"Let go of me."

Ramos laughed as tugged her hair harder. "Time to introduce me to your man."

---

*T*he moment Nick saw Leandra's text, calling herself 'wifey,' he knew he'd be changing the plan. She didn't scare easily, so whatever made her decide to change their backstory from partners to married, had to have spooked her, even if just a little.

Nick held his hands up while he stared down the wrong end of a weapon. This wasn't the first time, and he knew sure as shit, it wouldn't be the last.

"Take it easy, fellas," Nick said, eyeing the kitchen. His throat tightened as Ramos ran his fingers through Leandra's soft hair and then yanked hard enough it forced her to a standing position. "Get your boss out here and tell him to bring my wife." The word 'wife' rolled easily off his tongue.

A little too easy.

"Step up on the dock and keep your hands where we can see them," one of the guards said.

Nick did as instructed.

The guard that had been doing all the talking patted him down, finding his weapon.

Nick eyed Leandra as she stepped from the kitchen sliding glass doors, Ramos following two steps behind and obviously eyeing her backside. He couldn't decide if he should play the possessive, jealous hubby or the trusting one.

Or perhaps a little of both.

She smiled and waved, her feet moving a little faster than a normal walk. Ramos grabbed her arm, yanking her back.

Nick's blood heated, and he maneuvered toward the house, but the two guards lurched forward, aiming their weapons at his chest and head.

"Tell your men to stand down," Leandra said, breaking free from Ramos' grasp.

Ramos waved to his men. "Bring him to me." He leaned closer to her, pressing his hand on her back. "Take a seat at the patio table. Try anything and your husband dies." He pressed his index finger against his temple and cocked his thumb.

Nick strolled across the grass, his hands at his sides, one guard behind him, the other one next to him. Once inside the pool gate, Ramos greeted him, putting his body between Nick and Leandra. She stood to the side, making eye contact. Her steady gaze and her carefree body language indicated she wasn't concerned by the events, but he knew firsthand she'd become a master at masking her true emotions.

Except for lust, which was something he'd have to deal with later.

"I don't like strangers coming to my house uninvited," Ramos said. His eyes narrowed. "And I don't like business plans changing without notice."

"We had a planned meeting; I'm just early. Besides, my wife is your houseguest. Where she goes, I go." Nick knew changing the meet, making it a surprise, had the potential to backfire, but it would also give him the opportunity to gauge how desperate Ramos was to unload his merchandise as well as how badly he wanted Leandra. "And I didn't like what I saw in the kitchen, or what she told me about last night and your sexual advances and threats."

Leandra tilted her head. "He understands." Leandra's voice had a natural raspy sound. "Besides, you know I can take care of myself."

"Sorry, hon." Nick shrugged. "But I wasn't going to sit out there until eleven and watch you fend off advance after advance, much less have him pulling your hair." Nick inched closer to Ramos, puffing out his chest. "I'll kill you if you touch her again."

Ramos smiled. He carried himself with a heavy dose of arrogance. His power, however, wasn't exerted by his size or strength, but by the men he surrounded himself with. His muscle, so to speak. That was a good news/bad news situation. The good news was all Nick had to do was get this man out of his element, and he'd have the upper hand in seconds. The bad news was that right now, even with his brother and a few other men sprinkled around the lake and house, he was still outgunned, and he could only imagine how much manpower Ramos would bring when the deal went down.

"I don't like being watched." Ramos stood behind Leandra, his hand on her shoulder. "Or manipulated."

She shrugged it off.

Nick took a large step forward, but the guards shoved their guns in his face. "If you were in my shoes, you'd be watching me like a hawk."

"I wouldn't let my wife spend the night at another man's house."

Nick laughed. "As my wife said, she's perfectly capable of taking care of herself. The only reason she stayed was to get a good look at how you operate both personally and professionally. She was watching you more than I was from a distance." He made his way around the table, ignoring the protests of the guards. He caught a whiff of Leandra's shampoo. He couldn't wait for this to be over so he could have her...once. "We don't do business with just anyone."

"Neither do I," Ramos said, waving his hand at the table. "I don't like being lied to or manipulated. You showing up at my home unannounced doesn't make me want to do business with either of you."

Nick looped his arm around Leandra's waist. "Excuse me for a moment while I give my wife a proper hello." He leaned in, inhaling more of her tropical scent as it mixed with the fresh air. "Hey, hon." He pressed his mouth against hers, parting her lips with his tongue and taking a quick swirl around, enjoying the taste of bitter coffee mixed with bacon.

His body sizzled when she splayed her hands against his chest. "Hi, babe," she whispered.

Nick squeezed her ass before pulling away. "Let's discuss business now, since we're all here."

"You're a cocky son of a bitch." Ramos pulled out a chair and sat down, waving his hands to various people, who all jumped into action. "I like that."

"You don't get anywhere in life by being meek." Nick held back a chair for Leandra before settling next to her with his hand resting on her warm, sun-kissed thigh. "This deal has to go down tonight."

"Why is that?" Ramos asked as he lit up a cigar, offering one to everyone.

Nick shook his head. "Because Agent Fielding—"

"Agent Fielding is no one I'm concerned with." Ramos arched a brow, but his lips drew into a tight line.

"Don't play dumb." Nick shifted so the smoke didn't blow in his face, but it also put him even closer to Leandra. He didn't need to be so close that his knee touched hers, nor did his hands need to be on her body, but he couldn't resist the pull she had over him.

Didn't want to, either.

And that thought scared him more than dying if this operation went south.

"My sources tell me that Fielding is waiting on a search warrant for your warehouse."

"Under what pretense? I'm a model citizen." Ramos smiled, then winked.

"Your poker rooms."

"And how do you know this?" Ramos leaned back in his chair, crossing his ankle over his knee. Only the way he held his cigar, tight between his fingers instead of swirling it, told Nick that Ramos was nervous.

Leandra glanced between the two men. "I was on a fact-finding mission here, while Nick did his own gathering of intel, and if we don't do the deal tonight, it's not going to happen, and we disappear."

"I won't be strong-armed into a deal, and since my

men don't know about Fielding's plan, I don't believe Fielding is a threat."

"I thought you might say that." Nick pulled out his phone and pulled up the information he'd gotten directly from Fielding when Nick had approached him early this morning. "I have a man inside the FBI, and he gave me this." Nick pushed his phone across the table. "You've got a leak inside your operation who has been feeding the Feds, specifically Agent Fielding. My contact says we'll have a window of opportunity to move the merchandise tonight before Fielding homes in on your casino gig."

Ramos set the phone down, resting his elbows on the table. "I don't trust liars and don't believe I have a leak."

"If you don't want to do business, then we can walk," Leandra said, her hand resting on Nick's shoulder, massaging gently, making his body want to forget he had an operation to manage.

"I didn't say that." Ramos sucked on his cigar with his fat lips. "But I don't have a leak."

"You have one; otherwise, you wouldn't be in this predicament in the first place. Another reason I showed up unannounced." Nick rotated his neck, eyeing the house and yard. There really was a mole, but thus far, the intel he'd gathered hadn't netted much. Nick planned on changing that in less than twenty-four hours. "When this is all done, I'll hand you the mole on a silver platter."

"I don't need you to hand me anything," Ramos said, his voice laced with disdain.

"You need someone to move the merchandise before Fielding gets permission to legally poke around." Nick, reluctantly, took his hand off Leandra's thigh and folded his arms on the table. "I can move the merchandise and sell all of it before Fielding can wipe his ass from his morning shit."

"If I'm under investigation, and this agent has all this crap on me, why take the risk? Why not just let me crash and burn?"

Leandra sat up straighter, smoothing down her skirt and crossing her ankles.

God, she made Nick nuts.

"We have a buyer who wants consistent merchandise," Leandra said. "We'd like to help you increase your operation, making a hefty profit all around."

"Sounds like you've got this all planned out." Ramos flicked the ashes of his cigar. The breeze picked them up as they floated effortlessly toward the pool.

Nick nodded. "This is a win-win and could be the beginning of a long and prosperous relationship."

"Perhaps, but we don't have time for an auction." Ramos rubbed the back of his neck. "If what you say is true."

"It's true, and we don't need an auction," Nick said, leaning back, looping his arm over Leandra's shoulders. "We've got two buyers who are looking for slave labor, and they will take the entire lot."

"You don't even know what I have." Ramos sucked on his cigar, the tip turning red.

"We've been watching your operation for months now," Leandra said.

She'd gathered a fair amount of information on Ramos' operation, but what she hadn't found out, Nick's resources with the Aegis Network had uncovered in less than five hours. Even he was impressed by what they'd been able to uncover and put into place. Of course, some of Nick's old buddies had come through, making this a well-put-together op with the best of the best.

The plan still had a few holes, and any number of things could go wrong, but Nick wasn't going to focus on that.

"I want 1.5 million," Ramos said before he blew out his smoke, his lips forming a circular motion as he snapped his jaw, creating rings.

"Right now, we've got the buyers at a million. Best we're gonna get for this deal on short notice. But we can guarantee we'll be able to increase your fair market value by twenty percent in six months." All Nick needed to do was to get Ramos to agree to this sale. That way he could make sure all the current victims were moved to a safe location before slapping handcuffs on Ramos. But in the process, he needed to find out who Skyler had been sold to and help Leandra bring her home to her family.

Ramos put the cigar between his teeth and held out his hand. "If this deal goes off without a hitch, then we can discuss doing further business. If not?" He shrugged. "I'm going to fuck your beautiful wife while you watch, and then I'm going to kill you."

Nick knew Ramos believed his own words, but no way in hell, no matter what went down tonight, would Ramos ever be laying a finger on Leandra.

She belonged to Nick.

What the fuck? Where did that come from? Screw her once and she'd be out of his system. She was just another chick that reminded him he was a man with needs, not a man with desires.

Big difference.

At least that is what he told himself.

4

*L*eandra kicked off her shoes on the back porch of the house Nick had taken her to last night. In typical Florida fashion, the outside wasn't much to talk about with its chipped paint and over-grown landscaping. But the new hardwood floors in the kitchen and family room, and brand-new stainless-steel appliances, gave the house a modern, upscale feel-ing. The inside had been freshly painted with warm, neutral colors that brightened up the space when the sun filtered through the windows.

"Sorry about the married thing." She flopped herself down on the soft leather sofa. It felt cool against her legs, which had a thick layer of humidity covering her skin. "Not sure why I thought that would get him to stop hitting on me."

"I think it works to our advantage." Nick sat down on the far end of the couch, his legs stretching out over the coffee table. All morning long, his hands had been on her skin. The attention he showed her in front of Ramos had been above and beyond. However, once on the boat and out of sight of his men, Nick continued to caress her shoulders, or even hold her hand. He explained as he helped her from the boat to the dock that he was sure they were being followed, watched.

Maybe they were, but his affection felt more like desire than a show put on for the sake of a killer.

"Besides, I don't like the way he looks at you, much less how he pulled your hair."

"I can't say I liked it much either. He's a disgusting man."

Nick turned his head. His soft-blue eyes cast a concerned look as the sunlight beamed through the window. "Who wouldn't think twice about raping and killing you."

She shivered. Ever since Kent passed, she started taking risks she normally wouldn't. It wasn't a death wish but more like sticking her middle finger up at life. "I was definitely in over my head, so thanks." She bit down on her lower lip. The only thing worse than knowing she'd taken on more than she could cope with was having to admit it.

"You're welcome." The corners of his mouth tipped upward. "But I think you'd manage to land on your feet...like Cat Woman." He winked.

Without thinking, she kicked his thigh with her foot, letting her toes feel the hard muscles inside his jeans.

He grabbed her ankle, fanning his thumb over her sensitive skin, resting her foot on his leg.

She should pull away and shut down this insane attraction that had come out of nowhere.

"How long were you married?" he asked, his face turned serious, and his eyes filled with an understanding that made her heart beat faster.

"Just over two years."

"Had you known him long?"

"A year before we married," she said, letting out a long breath. Normally, she couldn't bring herself to talk about Kent with anyone, especially strangers, but Nick did something to her brain, making her want to share her sob story with him.

Perhaps misery loves company.

"Kent, my husband, was originally from the Bronx, and we met in a bakery when he managed to dump his jelly doughnut all over my white shirt." Her lungs burned at the memory. She'd been admiring his physique since he'd opened the door for her. She couldn't decide what she wanted, which was often the case, so she let him go first. When the clerk handed him his order, she suspected he'd go to the left, but instead he turned right, and she walked into him and his doughnut. "It was love at first stain."

Nick laughed. "First time I saw my wife, I thought my heart would stop beating. When she smiled at me, I was toast."

"If you don't mind me asking, how old were you when she died?"

He continued to caress her ankle and foot as if it were a normal thing to do while talking about their dead spouses.

"We were both twenty. Only been married for a few months."

"That's young."

He nodded, dropping his head to the sofa. "Most people think we got married because she was pregnant, but we'd planned our elopement two weeks before we found out. I lost her and our baby."

Leandra gasped, covering her mouth with both hands. She and Kent had decided to start trying to have children as soon as he returned home from his last deployment, only he never came home.

"I'm so sorry," she whispered.

"Thank you." He rolled his head and stared at her with a mixture of commiseration and intent, a contrast of emotions that only another survivor could comprehend. "A couple of months after she died, I enlisted. I couldn't stand to be near anything that reminded me of her."

"I can understand that."

"For a couple of years, I couldn't even look at another woman. Everyone told me I needed to move on. That Joanne would want me to."

"I'm getting that left and right, and it makes me nuts." But deep down, she knew there was a truth to the statements. "I'll be ready when I'm ready."

"If you think like that, you'll end up like me, and sometimes it's a very lonely headspace."

"Being a widow is a lonely place to be in general," she said, lifting her other foot to the couch and leaning back, resting her head on the side of the sofa.

Nick's fingers dug into her heels, massaging her aching feet. "My older brother, who you'll meet this afternoon, thinks I wear my pain as if it were burned onto my chest like a scarlet letter."

"My mother thinks I hold on to my grief out of fear." Talking about her late husband never seemed natural, much less comfortable, but Nick had a way of making her feel as though he understood why moving on was something that wasn't in her wheelhouse.

"Your mother could be right."

"Have you ever tried peeling the scarlet letter off?"

"No," he said, still rubbing her feet with strong fingers. "But I've learned to accept things as they are. I'll never love another woman, nor be in a lasting relationship, and I'm okay with that."

She moaned as he worked from her heels across her arches. "I want to be okay with that." Tossing her arm over her eyes, she tried to ignore the heat pulsing through her body. "I know I'll never find love again because I don't want it, but I'm tired of closing myself off to being a woman."

The sofa shifted as he pushed her one foot to the side. She jerked her head up as he settled between her legs.

Her body betrayed her as she let her knees fall outward, giving him plenty of room to nestle himself in her womanhood.

She sucked in a breath as his hands framed her face. Her arms wrapped around his broad shoulders.

"You're a beautiful woman." His lips brushed the tip of her nose. "Only way to be okay with having sex with someone else is to do it with someone who doesn't want or expect anything else from you."

"Is that what you did?" she asked.

He nodded. "I've wanted you since the moment I laid eyes on you."

"I was kind of turned on when you jumped me in the bathroom."

"That was really hot." He winked. "We have a few hours to kill while we wait around for everything and everyone to get into place."

"Here? Now?" Her panties moistened as he pressed against her. All her nerve endings went up in flames. "Aren't there people watching us?"

"Not inside the house." He frowned. Pressing his hands on the sofa, he lifted his chest up. "I'm sorry, this wasn't appropriate."

"Fuck appropriate," she muttered, wrapping her legs around his muscular ass. "This is a one-time thing."

"That's all I've got to give you."

"That's all I want," she said, and her nipples tightened. "I should warn you that I haven't had sex with anything other than my own fingers or vibrator—"

He covered her mouth with his, sucking her tongue inside, swirling his everywhere. Her nipples puckered against her bra, the fabric making them so hard it felt like they were on fire.

Kneeling, he kept the lustful kiss going as he scooped her up in his arms.

"Whoa...what are you doing?"

"I can't fuck you properly on that sofa, so I'm taking you to the bedroom."

She found his bluntness endearing. "I can walk." Being a little bit on the heavy side, men didn't carry her often, but Nick seemed to manage her as if she were a stack of feathers.

"When I'm done with you, walking might be a problem."

"I hope that's a promise." She pressed her lips on his ear, sucking his earlobe into her mouth.

He hissed as he kicked open the door to one of the bedrooms. Setting her feet down on the floor, he held her hips, staring into her eyes.

Her chest heaved up and down with each sharp breath. A combination of masculine musk and fresh soap smacked her nostrils, sending a tingle through her body. Until Kent, she hadn't been comfortable being naked in front of a man. Every lover she'd had before him somehow managed to make her feel as though her body imperfections made her less of a sensual woman. Most of the men hadn't meant to cause her feelings of insecurity, but their poor choice of words and actions left her feeling anything but sexy.

Kent made her feel as though she were the most perfect woman in the world, and not just physically.

The way Nick looked her over with his lust-filled eyes, licking his lips, spread a hot sizzle across her skin, igniting a passion so deep it rocked her soul. She swallowed as his palms cupped her breasts before his fingers magically unbuttoned her blouse.

With both his palms holding her breasts, he leaned over and kissed her neck. Her hands rested on his shoulders, her fingers dancing across his firm muscles. She tipped her head to the side, letting out a soft moan as he unfastened the front clasp of her bra.

His soft, moist lips kissed her nipple gently before he swirled his tongue over it, rolling and twisting the sensitive nub.

She clutched his head, running her fingers through his light-brown hair, watching him toy with her body. She couldn't remember the last time she felt this alive. Her heart beat so fast, she couldn't catch her breath.

He kissed his way down to the top of her skirt, his hands kneading her ass under the fabric. All she could think about was shoving his face between her legs, throwing one leg over his shoulder.

She shuddered.

The tearing of her zipper sent a warm tingle over her nerves. As he rolled her skirt down over her hips, a combination of fear and passion filled her mind. She stood there naked, in front of a man. A man who wasn't her husband. A man she should feel guilty about being with but didn't. Not one bit.

The way Nick kissed her inner thigh overwhelmed her. The thought she could actually like the man behind the lips sent her heart pounding erratically.

When he looked up at her, locking gazes, she gasped. His intense stare filled her with hot desire.

And maybe something akin to caring. No, just strong mutual appreciation. They shared a common pain. They had bonded on that level.

And they were hot for each other.

But that was it.

"Oh...my...God," she whispered as his tongue slid between her legs.

Gently, he pushed her onto the bed. His fingers and mouth caressing her with gentle strokes. His touch sweet and sensitive but demanding at the same time. His movements were slow and meticulous. Everything he did had purpose.

She moaned, running her fingers through his soft buzzed hair, tossing her head from side to side and digging her heels into the mattress. Her body tensed, floating on the edge of oblivion. A long, intense quiver, starting in the pit of her stomach, flowed toward where Nick's mouth connected to her as if he were sucking all her passion out of her.

A pang of guilt tickled the back of her mind. The guilt, however, wasn't what she'd expected. She thought this would feel more like cheating.

Not like letting go of the pain.

It wasn't that she was about to forget all about the love of her life, but being with Nick seemed to give her the will to do what she knew Kent would want her to do.

Live.

And she'd been merely existing.

Nick looked up at her, his eyes conveying the kind of hunger that would devour her with delicious torture. She watched as he kissed her intimately, his fingers gliding inside her, stroking her with the precision and passion a violinist used when striking the bow across the strings on his instrument.

His gaze never wavered, and she couldn't stop staring. Her lungs burned with each short breath she took. Everything about Nick made her want to give life… and love… a second chance.

He sucked harder on her swollen nub.

"Oh…my…God." She dropped her hands to her sides, fisting the sheets, her body rocking against his mouth, her toes curling as a guttural groan bellowed from her throat. Her orgasm hovered on the verge of breaking free. She wanted to slow it down. Take the time to let it build to a boil.

"Nick," she ground out behind gritted teeth. Clutching her thighs against the side of his head, she let out a husky groan.

Her body convulsed over and over. Moans came out of her mouth that she'd never heard before. It was the never-ending orgasm, quivering like the aftershocks of an earthquake. She blinked, staring at the fan swirling above her head, trying to take deep calming breaths. Her pulse raced out of control as he gently kissed her, gliding his lips to her inner thigh, then stomach.

Orgasms generally came easy to her, but never had they come on so fast and furious that she couldn't manage to hold them off for long moments. Then again, for the last two years, she'd been giving them to herself.

"You taste like sunshine and whiskey." He got to his knees and raised her leg, kissing her ankle as his hand glided down her calf. "It's addicting."

"We need to get you out of your clothes," she whispered. "It's only fair."

"Well, since your twisting my arm." He lifted his shirt over his head and tossed it to the floor.

Biting on her lower lip, she scooted to a sitting position and ran her fingers across his firm chest. His muscles twitched at her touch. When she kissed his neck, running her fingers over his nipples, he made a hissing noise that rolled across her skin like a blanket of warm lotion. Wanting to touch him in the most intimate way, she fiddled with the buckle and eased the belt through the loops, tossing it to the floor.

She hadn't wanted to feel good, or make someone else feel good, in so long. It created a hunger that burned through her veins.

He batted her hands away and stood at the end of the bed, lowering his pants over his hips. He paused, reaching in his back pocket and pulling out his wallet. He unfolded the leather case, taking something out. When he tossed the condom on the bed, warm goosebumps floated to the top of her skin.

Holding her breath, she felt the corners of her mouth tip into a small smile as he revealed himself. She swallowed. She'd seen a few naked men in her day, but

Nick's body was like a temple meant to be worshiped with his broad frame and long lean legs. His tight stomach narrowed at the hips.

And the rest of him?

Wow.

Sitting on the edge of the bed, she splayed her fingers across his stomach, feeling the muscles contract under her touch. She rubbed her hands up to his hard nipples, enjoying how he groaned when she let her fingernails graze them. She leaned in and kissed him just above the belly button. His hardness pressed inside her cleavage. Resisting the urge to squeeze her breasts together, she leaned back a little, taking him into her hands.

The way he gently brushed her hair out of the way, holding it back with his hands, sent a warm rush of blood to every erogenous zone she had.

Sucking the tip into her mouth, she stroked him, enjoying his groans and the way he fingered her hair. She felt admired, something she hadn't felt from a man in a long time. She took more of him in her mouth, swirling her tongue over the tip.

He reached down with one hand and twisted her nipple, igniting a fire deep inside her.

She moved over him with quick thrusts of her mouth, her fingers caressing what she couldn't take. The desire to please him filled her mind and soul.

"Christ," he muttered as he pulled at her hair, almost trying to tug her away from him.

She ignored his efforts.

"Leandra," he said, followed by a deep growl.

Slowly, she glided her lips from him. Stroking him with her hands she looked up at him and smiled. "What?"

"I need you to slow down." He arched a brow.

"You mean like this?" She kissed the tip, spreading her tongue over it before gliding just the head inside her mouth with very little pressure, repeating the action a couple of times, watching his eyes roll up under his eyelids. The power she felt over him was intoxicating.

"I think this might be worse."

"Worse?" She squeezed him, letting her teeth graze his sensitive skin.

"That's not how I meant it." He tugged her hair a little harder, forcing her neck back. "You have maybe two minutes before I toss you on your back and I make good with what I said last night."

"Remind me what you said?" Her smile spread wide across her face, and her eyes twinkled with mischief.

He groaned. "That I'm going to fuck you like there is no tomorrow."

---

*N*ick had completely lost his mind.

Not to mention his body.

Leandra had been more than he could have anticipated. He knew taking her to bed would probably rock his world. But staring down at her now, with his cock buried in her mouth, rocking his world was the under-statement of the century.

She'd blown it right the fuck up.

And not just with sex.

He found himself wondering what it would be like to have dinner with her, staring at her across the table, holding her hand, talking about random things, and enjoying every second of her company.

He groaned as her teeth grazed his skin again.

Damn tease and she knew it.

And he loved it.

"That's it," he said with a growl, tugging on her hair, careful not to pull too hard. He didn't want to hurt her. The vision of Ramos yanking it filtered through his mind. He'd kill the motherfucker if he ever touched her again.

Taking a deep breath, he pushed the rage from his mind and focused on the beautiful woman now standing in front of him.

He eyed her voluptuous body, mentally taking a picture of every curve. He traced his finger from her lips to her full breasts, circling each nipple, smiling as they puckered into tight, tiny nubs. He continued down her stomach and across to each hip.

Her smile lightened up the room and awoke his aching heart.

His breath hitched and he froze. The room spun with the swirling of the fan. He squeezed her hips to steady himself. The familiar sensation of affection wiggled its way into his mind. Sure, he liked the women he went to bed with. Respected them. Valued them as human beings, but he never felt any deep emotional connection to them. Purely physical.

Appreciation? Yes.

Affection? No.

"What's wrong?" she asked, her voice echoing with a sudden insecurity that filled him with a sense of anguish because he'd caused it.

Looping his arms around her waist, he drew her close, letting himself slide between her legs, feeling her warmth trickle over him, reminding himself that she didn't want him for any other reason than she needed to allow herself to be a woman again.

He swallowed, focusing on the undeniable sexual heat between them.

Not the feelings she rustled deep inside his core.

"Nothing." He kissed her temple, cupping her full ass in his hands. "You're fucking gorgeous," he stammered out. "You took my breath away." It certainly wasn't a lie, but if he wasn't careful, she was the kind of woman that could rebuild his heart... and then crush it.

Her hands roamed down his back, over his hips, and across his stomach. He shuddered, grabbing her wrist before she could curl her glorious fingers around his shaft.

She cocked her head and smiled. "Can't handle it?" she asked.

He groaned, knowing he couldn't. Any other woman he'd been with, he could have. Sex had become an exercise in mental control and physical release.

Being with her had turned into an exercise of control, only not his, because he had none.

"I can't," he said softly. An admittance that humbled him. He cupped her breast, leaning over to suck it into his mouth.

Her soft moans filled the room, echoing through his mind, wreaking havoc on his body. If he entered her sweetness now, it would be over before it began.

Kissing her nipples, he pushed her back on the bed and reached between their bodies. He ran his finger over her hard nub, gliding inside her warmth with three fingers, curling them at the top.

He devoured each breast as he stroked her, occasionally slipping his fingers out to rub her clit in a quick, circular motion. Her hips rolled with his hand as she quietly called out his name. Hearing his name float off her tongue sent a long shiver from his toes to his head, spreading heat to all his nerve endings.

His control finally snapped. Reaching for the condom, he tore it open. His hands trembled as he tried to cover himself. Putting on protection had never been difficult before.

"Fuck," he whispered, trying again.

Only this time her sweet fingers covered his, and she eased the condom over his length.

A deep growl built from the pit of his stomach. He eased between her legs, his hands cupping her face as he slowly glided himself into her. Tighter than expected, he had to grit his teeth to stop himself from climaxing right then and there.

She wrapped her legs around his waist, her hands roaming his back and ass, her fingers digging into his muscles.

His vision blurred. For a long moment, he stayed still, staring into her mesmerizing dark eyes. There was so much passion behind the chocolate pools, it caused his heart to swell with something akin to deep abiding affection.

An understanding of her heart and mind filled his brain. He tried to convince himself that this connection was only because of their shared loss, but deep down he knew she'd managed to reach inside all those places he'd hidden from the world for the last ten years.

He fanned her soft, rosy cheeks with his thumbs. "You're an incredible woman."

Her eyes widened as a smile slowly appeared on her angelic face.

On the inside, he scrambled to protect himself from the kind of heartache that would destroy him. On the outside, he rammed his tongue inside her mouth, filling it with all the lust he had for her.

And he did lust after her in the most primal way.

Rolling his hips, he swallowed all her sweet moans. He wanted to bring her to climax before he lost himself completely, and that would be sooner than he liked.

She ground herself against him, and he bit down on her lower lip as his toes curled. He could no longer contain himself. He raised up on his hands, staring down at her while her head rolled back and forth.

"Help me," he murmured, taking her hand, placing it

between their bodies, pressing her fingers against herself.

She blinked her eyes open.

"That's it, hon," he whispered, thrusting himself deep inside her. He leaned over, sucking her nipple all the way in his mouth.

She hissed, arching her back. "Yes," she said with a throaty pant. "Oh, my...Nick!"

Her body rocked, shaking the bed as if it were a waterbed and they'd jumped into it together. She grabbed his ass with both hands, pulling him in deeper.

He collapsed on top of her, burying his face in her neck as he thrust his hips hard and fast until he swelled inside her and exploded. His entire body shivered. Every inch of his skin burned with exquisite flames. Sucking on her neck, he tried to control the dizziness that threatened to overtake him.

He'd gotten drunk on her.

Worse, he was addicted to her.

He shivered again. His brain worked to squelch his crazy thoughts while his heart tried to keep from accepting the rush of those emotions that would surely be the death of him.

Long moments passed as their breathing slowly returned to normal.

But there was nothing normal about this encounter, and Nick found himself in a situation where he wanted to push her away. He could easily say something so insensitive that she'd never want to look at him again.

He'd learned from his little brother, Ramey, how to hurt a woman with a single sentence.

Ten of those sentences filled his mind.

But he couldn't use them. Or wouldn't use them. It didn't matter because he was her first fuck after the death of her dearest husband, and Nick, of all people, knew what that meant.

He should be grateful that she'd thank him for the good time and be on her way.

The click of a lock ripped him from his thoughts. Her jerked his head up.

"You heard that, too," she whispered.

"I did." Propping himself up, he reached over the bed, lifting the curtain a tad. "Fuck."

"What?" She gripped his shoulders, staring at him with those damn, intoxicating eyes.

"My brother is here." He kissed her lips, letting his tongue glide over them.

"Nick? Where the hell are you?" his brother, Logan, yelled.

Nick had no desire to get up. He enjoyed being on top of Leandra and in her, a fact his body was all too well aware of.

The doorknob to the bedroom rattled. "You in here? Where's the PI?"

"We'll be right out."

Leandra tucked her head into his chest. "Did you have to say we?" she whispered.

"I'll come in," Logan said.

"Open that fucking door and I'll tell Mom you were the one who broke her antique vase."

"We were barely teenagers then. I'm sure Mom is over it," Logan said.

The door shook.

Nick grabbed some plastic decorative thing shaped like a sailor off the nightstand. Turning his body, making sure not to cause Leandra any pain, he hurled the object at the door. "I said I'd be out in a minute, asshole."

The decorative statue hit the door with a resounding thud, then dropped to the floor.

"Well, hurry up. We've got a human trafficking ring to take down and a young girl to find," Logan yelled.

Nick cupped Leandra's shocked, stricken face. "I'm sorry. All my brothers are assholes."

"This is so embarrassing."

It wasn't the first time Nick had gotten caught with his pants down. Seemed it was a tradition with the Sarich boys.

"Not to mention unprofessional," she said, her hands massaging his shoulders, easing any tension that had seeped into his muscles. "We're in the middle of a case."

He nodded, though he didn't agree with the unprofessional part. He'd done his job by finding her and letting her father know she was safe. Going after Ramos, he was doing on his own time, though he had the full backing of the Aegis Network, using resources not currently in the field, along with calling in a few favors. "We needed our rest during what little down-time we're going to have once this plan is in motion."

She laughed. "You call what we did rest?"

"You are very relaxed, aren't you?"

The smile that spread across her face tickled his senses. "You better get off me." She squeezed herself around his growing erection.

He groaned but carefully maneuvered himself to the side, covering her sexy body in the sheet. "Take your time getting dressed." He kissed her nose. "I'll go deal with my dickhead brother."

He stood, glancing around the floor for his clothes. They seemed to be all over the place. He gathered them up, tossing his shirt and belt on the end of the bed before hiking up his pants. When he looked up, he paused as he pulled up the zipper.

Leandra had propped herself against a stack of pillows, her hands clasped behind her head, and she bit down on her lower lip. The sheet fell over her breasts but barely covered them.

"Enjoying yourself?" he asked.

She nodded.

"Keep looking at me like that and we'll just have to fuck again in the very near future."

"I think it's a moral imperative at this point." She winked.

"Christ," he muttered. "You're gonna be the death of me." He snagged his shirt, turned on his heels, and marched himself right out of the bedroom.

That woman was more than dangerous.

And having her again would be a mistake.

But he knew he'd never be able to resist her.

He wasn't sure what was more disturbing, the seductive hold she had over him or the shitty grin on his brother's face when Nick strolled into the family room. "That was a dick move." He glared at his brother.

Logan stood in the middle of the room, his hands planted on his hips. "I didn't know she was in there with you. Last we talked, she was with Ramos."

Nick scowled. Of all his brothers, Logan had been on Nick's ass to stop feeling sorry for himself and start living again, specifically, to be open to a relationship with a woman. "Not the point. You're totally embarrassed Leandra. I get messing with me, but you don't even know her."

Logan scratched the back of his head. "I honestly didn't know she was with you."

"You owe her an apology."

"Well, shit. You're hung up on a woman," Logan said matter-of-factly. "That's why you're so upset."

"I'm upset because you acted like a dick."

"You wouldn't care if you didn't have some kind of feelings for the woman, outside of wanting to get laid."

"Shut up," Nick said softly, looking over his shoulder. "She's in the other room."

"Wow." Logan shook his head. "She must be something to have gotten your panties in a wad."

The bedroom door squeaked open.

Nick narrowed his eyes. "Behave."

Logan grinned from ear to ear but nodded.

When Leandra waltzed down the small corridor and into the family room, Nick swallowed his breath.

Her long, still a little messy, hair flowed down over her large breasts, which bounced gracefully with her long strides. Her sweet smile slightly stifled, but when she locked gazes with him, her eyes twinkled like one of those sparklers on the Fourth of July.

"Leandra, this is my brother, Logan. He's going to act as one of our buyers."

"I appreciate your help on this," Leandra said with a strong and steady voice, but her cheeks flushed.

Nick rested his hand on the small of her back, guiding her to the sofa, ignoring his brother's arched brow. Nick didn't have girlfriends. He didn't even have friends with benefits.

He had sex.

Occasionally.

Between missions.

It wasn't like he went around screwing every woman in sight, nor did he ever treat them badly, only it was rare he ever went back to the same woman.

Much less showed affection of any kind in front of people.

"Have we heard from Ramos?" Logan asked, sitting in the oversized leather chair in the corner under the front window. Before he'd gotten back with his high school sweetheart, Logan had many short-lived relationships, but they always ended because Logan didn't think he could ever fall in love.

All the Sarich boys had issues with love, only Nick's

came from experiencing the ultimate pain of having that love destroyed by a senseless act.

"We're meeting him at his place." Nick sat next to Leandra, trying desperately not to touch her, but his fingers twitched. He'd spent the last ten years hiding in the military, taking every assignment and deployment he could. He volunteered for everything, which made it easy for him to avoid relationships.

"Dylan and a few of his buddies joined our team at Ramos' house."

"Who's Dylan?" she asked.

"Our little brother." Nick tossed his arm over the back of the sofa, a movement that wasn't lost on his brother, who cracked an all-knowing smile.

Nick hated that smile.

"When did he roll into town?" Nick asked.

"He's been in Orlando, only I didn't know it. Some special detail with NASA," Logan said. "When I reached out to some buddies, one of them happened to be working the same op with Dylan. They just wrapped up and were enjoying a day or two off."

"How many Sarich brothers are there?" Leandra crossed her sexy, muscular legs, tucking her hands between them.

Nick bit back a groan. He had no idea how he'd get through the next twenty-four hours without having a constant semi-erection. Everything about her turned him on. "Four of us. Dylan's with Delta Force now, and Ramey is a test pilot with the Army, currently living the dream in the desert."

"Impressive," Leandra said as she leaned forward to pick up her buzzing cell phone. "It's Ramos."

"Answer it." Nick leaned closer. "Put it on speaker."

"Hello?"

"Hello, baby," Ramos' voice echoed across the room. "How's the sexy lady? You feeling like a little phone fun?"

Nick fisted his hand as he swallowed hard. The desire to punch Ramos scorched his skin.

"What do you want?" Leandra placed her warm hand over Nick's, rubbing her thumb across his tight fist. Her sensitive touch only reminded him that he'd developed a sense of fierce protection toward her that went beyond duty, honor, and loyalty.

"Aww, can't talk dirty because Nicky-boy is right there with you?"

Nick could picture his fingers tightening around Ramos' neck, feeling his pulse slowly fade to nothing. He glanced toward his brother, who arched a brow.

"Is there a reason for this call? If not, we'll see you in a couple of hours," Leandra said with a cool tone, one Nick had to admire. Her strong, confident personality had to be the biggest turn on.

"Your husband was right about the leak."

Fielding hadn't given up his source inside Ramos' organization, so whoever it was could be in grave danger.

Not good.

"My husband is right about most things." Leandra

continued to squeeze his hand, only he wasn't sure if it was to calm him.

Or her.

Nick let out a long breath, trying to ignore his brother's glare of either concern or amusement. Didn't matter. Logan was going to have a field day with this after the op was over.

"I'm told that Fielding needs more evidence to warrant the search, so it could be a few more days."

Leandra's eyes went wide. "We still need to move the merchandise tonight."

"Agreed," Ramos said. "I was thinking it would be better if you rode with me rather than with your husband."

Logan pointed to his wrist, then waved his hand in front of his neck.

"Not going to happen," Leandra said, nodding in Logan's direction. "Now if you'll excuse me, I have a few things to take care of before we exchange money for merchandise."

She tapped the phone, then leaned back on the sofa. She scrolled through her email, and one caught her eye. "I've got an email from Nick Manovich."

"What?" Nick asked. "That's my alias, and I didn't send you anything."

She tapped on the attachment, which opened the PDF. She resized the document, and her pulse shot up when she realized what she was looking at. "These are the blueprints for the warehouse." She held the phone up to Nick. "And a list of titled merchandise, which has nothing to do with the business run out of that building."

Nick snagged the phone from her hands. "That's got to be from the agent working undercover."

"I think you're right." Leandra pointed to the signature line which read: *This is what you'll need for tonight... a friendly...*

Nick tossed the phone toward his brother, who caught it midair. "Can you get Mia to hack into Ramos' shit and this email account, and maybe decipher the names and descriptions on that list?"

Logan nodded.

"Who's Mia?" Leandra asked.

"My fiancé and she's about the best hacker in the world," Logan said with pride. "She'll have this done in a matter of minutes."

Nick swallowed his breath but at the same time puffed out his chest. The way Leandra handled herself with Ramos, and her determination to get the job done, had impressed Nick long before he'd snatched her from Ramos' house.

"Mia's a great hacker, but in battle, I'm glad I've got Leandra to watch my back."

Did he just fucking say that?

"Are you implying your girl is better than mine?" Logan laughed, pointing toward Leandra, then tapped his neck. "Aren't we a little old to be marking our territory?"

"What!?" Leandra twisted her body. "You didn't?" She rubbed her neck, her sexy gaze locked with his.

Nick brushed her hair to the side, staring at the spot on her neck just under her earlobe where he remembered sucking as hard as he could in the throes of passion, leaving a giant, dark-red hickey. Something he hadn't done since he'd been in high school.

"I kind of did." Nick cupped the side of her neck, rubbing his thumb over the mark. He wasn't proud of it, necessarily.

But he was proud of the woman who sat next to him.

"Wonderful," she said quietly.

For a moment, Nick forgot all about his brother as he leaned in and brushed his lips across hers in a brief, but tender kiss.

"How bad is it?" she questioned.

"Let's just say there is no way to cover it up." Nick told himself to pull away, but his heart pounded in a way it hadn't in years, and he'd be damned if he didn't admit he liked it.

Or that it felt good.

"Consider it a play on being married," Logan said, jostling Nick out of his trance. "What is up with the married cover anyway?"

"Quickest way I could think of for Leandra to bring me on as her partner." Nick continued to stare into Leandra's eyes, getting lost in her dark pools of warm honey, making him turn all gooey like an excited puppy.

She curled her fingers around his wrist while his hand still cupped her neck. He studied her face, wondering if she could ever move beyond the pain of her past.

He blinked. What was he thinking? He hadn't moved on, and he probably never would.

"I think the hickey sealed that cover," Logan said, laughing.

It sealed more than that, Nick thought.

$\mathcal{T}$he sun disappeared behind the horizon, leaving a fiery glow across the Florida sky. Leandra never thought she'd enjoy the south, but if she were being honest with herself, she missed it.

Even the damn heat.

The only reason she'd moved back north was to be near her family for their support after Kent had passed, but she'd fallen in love with the south almost as much as she loved Kent.

She sat next to Nick in the front seat of a dark-colored luxury SUV. Logan was situated in the back. She found their relationship to be filled with a loving angst that only brothers could share. Of course, she had no idea, considering she had no siblings herself, and neither had her husband.

She loved their sarcastic banter and was humbled by the way Logan seemed to drop everything to help his brother, which in turned helped her, and that thought gave her a warm shiver. She understood why Nick's brother had his back, but why did Nick have hers? The thought he might care about her sent a different kind of shiver across her body.

She'd fallen so hard and fast for Kent that she'd barely had a chance to catch her breath before she found herself walking down the aisle in a white dress on her father's arm.

Stealing a glance at Nick, her breath hitched. He looked her way and smiled. Her heart pounded so fast against her chest she figured it had jostled her breasts.

Nick pulled the SUV into a parking garage about five miles from the warehouse where Agent Fielding and his team had set up a meet to go over their part of the plan.

"You really think this is a good idea?" Leandra asked. Her interaction with the FBI had always been antagonistic in nature. Being a PI wasn't always valued by various law enforcement agencies.

Not to mention, she had a tendency to bend the law.

Just a tad.

Nick backed into the designated spot, across from three dark government cars. "I don't like bringing in the Feds, but he's got a man in Ramos' camp, and we need to know who that is and how to protect him."

Logan shifted in the back seat. "They had Ramos dead to rights on the casinos, but until Leandra here showed up, almost nothing on the trafficking, at least from what we've dug up on their investigation."

"According to Fielding and his agency," Leandra muttered. "Don't you think it's a little strange they had an inside guy for this long and he barely knew about the human trafficking ring?"

"The thought crossed my mind," Nick said.

"I'm happy to help take this asshole down, but I don't want them getting in the way of me finding my client's daughter, or trying to shut me out." Leandra reached out and touched Nick's forearm. "I'm not stopping until I find her."

He curled his long fingers over hers. His gentle smile sucker punched her lungs.

She swallowed.

"Neither am I." He stared into her eyes with such deep intent it made everything around her blur.

Except him.

"Thank you," she said softly.

"Mia hasn't been able to decipher the merchandise list, which also makes me skeptical that maybe it's a distraction," Logan said, snapping Leandra from her trance. "And worries me that Fielding is in contact with the agent, who might be giving us a line of crap."

"What does she say about the email?" Nick asked.

"She's still tracing it back to…" Logan paused for a moment… "something about finding the IP address where the email was created and tracking it through that."

Leandra nodded. "Any luck getting blueprints of the warehouse from the town?"

Nick rested his hand over hers. She stared at his

thumb caressing her skin. It had a calming effect on her mind, but the opposite in her heart.

She'd felt this intense pull once before.

Jerking her hand away, she turned her head and stared at the concrete wall.

"I should have them shortly, and Dylan has a guy who will compare them with what you were sent and let us know any discrepancies," Nick said. His tone had remained even, but she thought she heard a hint of disappointment.

Or maybe she made that up.

Focus on the case.

Another SUV backed into the spot next to them. A tall man with the same smile as Nick stepped from the vehicle. Tall was an understatement. He wasn't quite as broad as the other two brothers, but he had the same confident swagger as he strolled toward the car.

Nick hit the button that rolled down the passenger and rear side window.

"This must be Leandra. I'm Dylan, the tallest and best-looking of the Sarich brothers."

Both Nick and Logan coughed.

"Correction," Nick said. "Meet Baby Dyl who has yet to hit puberty."

"Screw you, hickey boy."

Leandra's cheeks went hot as she covered the mark on the side of her neck, which she realized wasn't the side that Dylan stood on, which meant he hadn't seen it...but knew about it.

"Christ, Logan," Nick muttered. "You've got a big fucking mouth."

Dylan laughed. "Yeah, he does. But I enjoyed telling Mom you got a girl in your life. She's planning your children's names right now."

"You've got to be kidding me," Nick said under his breath.

"Kidding you? I just entered the goddamned twilight zone," Leandra said, glaring at Nick, who had the audacity to shrug. "And this"—she pointed to her neck—"does not make me your girl."

"When a Sarich leaves his mark—"

She poked the center of Nick's chest with her index finger.

"Ouch." He smiled as he rubbed his chest. "That's going to leave a mark. Does that mean—"

"Oh, my God. You're impossible." Leandra's embarrassment quickly turned to amusement, which didn't make sense and sent her stomach on a roll. "Really? You had to give me a hickey?" She looked over her shoulder, giving Logan the evil eye. "And you had to tell your brothers?"

Turning her attention to the youngest man, she waved her finger at him. "What is wrong with you people?"

"You have to understand he was known as Hickey Boy in high school," Logan said, laughing. "It was like he saw a neck and had to suck."

"At least I didn't get caught by my girlfriend's father in nothing but my birthday suit right after having sex for the first time," Nick said with a dark and playful tone.

"No, you just got caught by Dad in the patrol car with your ass in the air," Dylan said with a stupid smile.

Leandra opened her mouth, but no words came out. Only a high-pitched screech.

"This coming from the guy who sent his crazy ex-girlfriend a dick pic who then preceded to plaster it all over Facebook," Nick said.

"Oh…my…God. Is the other Sarich boy as perverted as you three?" She blinked a few times, staring in Nick's warm blue eyes, wondering why the hell she found their banter endearing.

"We're not perverts," they said in unison.

"And Ramey is worse," Nick said.

"I used to hate being an only child, now I'm tickled pink," she said, her hand still covering the hickey.

"More like a dark red," Nick said.

She punched him in the shoulder.

"Ouch, geez, hon." He rubbed his arm. "Are you trying to brand me?"

"Yes." That was not the answer she expected to come out of her mouth.

"Sorry about my butthead brothers." Nick smiled, curling his fingers around her wrist. "But I can't say I'm sorry about anything else."

The brothers laughed.

She shook her head. "I imagine there are no secrets in your family."

"Nope." Nick rested his hand on her leg, his fingers

entwined with hers. The weirdest part of the entire conversation was that it didn't feel weird. Nor did holding his hand while his brothers exchanged funny glances.

She glanced across the parking lot and stared at the dark sedans. "Why are they still sitting in their cars?"

"I suspect trying get us tossed off, officially," Dylan said, resting his arm against the window.

"So much for wanting our help," Leandra said.

"They wanted our intel," Nick said. His touch was like a feather floating in the air.

"They want my team to stand down," Dylan said. "But that isn't going to happen. We're so much better at this than those idiots are, and if the Aegis Network can get officially hired, then we just become a part of that, and we can show the FBI how it's done."

"Is everything a pissing contest with men?" Leandra shook her head.

"Pretty much." Nick tapped her thigh, then pointed across the parking lot as six men, all in dark suits and all wearing wires in their ears, stepped from their vehicles.

"Why do I feel like I just went from *The Twilight Zone* to *Men in Black*?" she asked under her breath.

Dylan opened the car door, but Nick grabbed her arm. "We'll be out in a sec," he said.

She let out a long breath. "We need to get out there. The clock is ticking."

He nodded. "I wanted to apologize properly for the way I behaved, along with my brothers. It's just that our mom has had it in her head that we all need to get married and have babies. For years we've enjoyed harassing and tossing each other under the bus with our mom to deflect her constantly telling us we need good women in our lives."

She cocked her head. "And you boys tell your mother everything?"

"No, but my mom has got a blind date set up for Dylan tomorrow night, and he's using this op to get out of it and that hickey to deflect attention from him to me."

"You do realize you're all grown men, right?"

He laughed, squeezing her hand. "You'll understand when you meet my mother."

Before she could say another word, he was out the door. She pushed hers open and followed him across the parking garage where Dylan had pulled out a map and was pointing at it while the other men stood around him and nodded.

She'd deal with the idea of meeting his mother another time.

"Leandra?" a shorter man said as he stepped from the crowd, his hand stretched forward. "I'm Agent Fielding and while we're not thrilled by how you came about your intel, we appreciate it."

"Just doing my job."

"Now let us do ours." Fielding's voice rang out with an authoritative and aggressive tone.

Leandra arched a brow as she planted her hands on her hips, noticing that all the Sarich brothers had stopped talking and focused their attention on her. "All right, but if you think I'm sitting this one out, you've got another thing coming."

"You're a civilian, and this a federal operation."

"Being headed by a private civilian team," Nick said. "One you agreed to work with."

Leandra appreciated him coming to her defense, but she didn't need him to.

"I didn't agree to working with a PI who has no background in law enforcement." Fielding raised his chin.

"Yes, you did," Nick said, but she stepped in front of him.

"I'm not going anywhere but in that warehouse as planned, so let's just move forward, shall we?" she asked.

"Happy to, as soon as you leave." Fielding pointed to the SUV she'd rode in.

Leandra opened her mouth, but Nick spoke before she could.

"She's an integral part of our plan." Nick stood next to her, his hand pressing against the small of her back. He stared down at Fielding. "If I walk in there without her as my business partner in this deal, the entire plan falls apart, and we'll have a shitstorm on our hands, and I'm not good with that. We stick with the plan we presented you."

"Your plan, not ours, and we've made some changes." Fielding rolled on his feet, as if to make himself taller.

"What kind of changes?" Leandra asked, fisting her hands.

"We're not at liberty to share with you, so please, we need you to leave so we can discuss the new plans."

"Like hell," Nick said. "She's—"

Leandra raised her hand, covering Nick's mouth. "I'm the sole reason you've got anything on Ramos' trafficking. I'm the one who brought these fine men and their teams in, so back the fuck up. I'm going in with Nick, and you can't stop me."

"Yes, I can," Fielding said with a stupid grin. "I'll arrest you."

Dylan laughed. "Try it and I'll have my boss call your boss, and I think we know how that will turn out."

Nick tugged her hand from his mouth, dropping their entangled fingers to the side. She should pull away, but she wouldn't.

Or maybe she couldn't.

"Look, fellas," Nick said, giving her hand a good squeeze. "We invited you into this sting, and you're welcome to stay and play, but we've got operatives in the field, with a plan, ready to go."

Fielding shook his head, shoving his fists in his pockets. "This one is a dangerous woman with a death wish, and our agent tells us she's a loose cannon."

"That's bullshit," Leandra said behind gritted teeth. "Whoever your agent is has only seen or known me for less forty-eight hours and doesn't know dick about me."

"Who's the agent?" Nick leaned forward, forcing Fielding to look up at him.

Leandra bit back a smile, enjoying that a little too much.

"I won't compromise my agent's cover."

"You mean her cover," Logan said as he took the five steps from the government car. "The one you had send all the intel we have right now to Leandra."

"Alicia?" Leandra mentally went over every encounter she'd had with the woman, which wasn't many.

Logan nodded. "Just heard back from Mia." He pointed to Fielding. "Why would your agent send us intel from Nick's alias and a bogus email?"

"That's where you got the blueprints of the ware-house?" Fielding took a slight step back but still held his ground. "What makes you think we sent anyone an email?"

"Because my fiancé is the best ethical hacker in the world, so she knows her shit," Logan said with a protective tone.

"Why the hell would you do that without telling us?" Nick shook his head.

Leandra's mind turned over the events of the last forty-eight hours. Alicia had been at the house when Leandra had arrived, and immediately Leandra had assumed she and Ramos were lovers. Alicia had been nice enough, but she'd made it clear she didn't like Leandra's presence. "Her demeanor changed toward me from last night to this morning."

"That's because we told her who you were as soon as Nick contacted us," Fielding said, scratching his head.

"How did she change?" Nick asked, tilting her chin toward him with his thumb.

"Standoffish to 'I want to kill that bitch.' I assumed it was because of how badly Ramos wanted up my skirt right in front of her."

"Why would that bother my agent?" Fielding asked.

"It looked to me like they were fucking." Leandra enjoyed the way Fielding's eyes widened from her bluntness.

"I doubt that. Just playing her undercover part," Fielding said, but he obviously took Leandra's words to heart. "We never told her to send you anything. We have a secure method of communication."

"Fuck," Leandra said.

"Are you thinking what I'm thinking?" Nick asked, staring at her with knowing eyes.

"If you're thinking that Alicia has been turned, then yeah." She grabbed Nick by the arm, yanking him toward Dylan who stood next to the hood of a car where the blueprints had been laid out. "And either this is all bullshit information, and they've moved the merchandise or—"

"It's an ambush," Nick said.

"Well, you know what they say about that?" Dylan asked, smiling.

"You attack it head on," both Logan and Nick said

with a little more excitement than she would have thought appropriate.

"First off," Fielding said as he stepped between Leandra and Dylan. "You're not attacking anything, and second off, our agent hasn't flipped."

"You don't know that," Leandra said, her blood pumping through her body with a sense of urgency. "Regardless, if our covers have been compromised, we need to get in there and fast, or all those young people are going to be lost forever." Not to mention, she may never find out where Skyler had been sold to, breaking her promise to the young girl's parents.

"And you don't know she has." Fielding puffed out his chest.

Dylan tapped his earpiece. "I need a visual on Ramos, and I also need an accounting of activity at the warehouse. And where the fuck are the blueprints from the city?"

"Stand down," Fielding shouted. "I will have all of you arrested for interfering with an investigation."

"Good luck with that," Dylan said, rolling up the blueprints. "You're either on board with us and do things our way, or you can sit back, watch, and maybe learn a thing or two."

"You arrogant little prick," Fielding said.

"That I am," Dylan said. "Leandra, are you ready to roll?"

"I was born ready."

"That's my girl," Nick said, looping his arms over her shoulders and kissing her cheek.

His warm lips burned her already flushed skin. She turned, giving him her best glare.

He just smiled and traced the hickey on her neck with his forefingers.

"All right, Boy Wonder, let's go." Leandra laughed as Nick's expression turned from a smile to a frown.

"I'm Batman. Dylan over there is Boy Wonder," Nick said.

Out of the corner of her eye, she saw Fielding talking on his phone and waving his hands wildly while he tossed out a few curses. "He's not going to let us walk out of here."

"He's not going to have a choice," Logan said, holding up his phone. "Our boss just got the FBI to hire the Aegis Network to run a search and rescue mission, and we've been authorized to bring in Dylan and his Delta Force team while they are on a few days leave. Fielding's hands are tied, though we're going to have to work with him since he's the one with the authority to bring Ramos in."

Fielding tapped his phone before shoving it in his pocket. "You better not fuck up this arrest for me." He pointed to Leandra.

She smiled sweetly. "You stay out of my way; I'll stay out of yours."

"We'll stick with the original plan, but..." Fielding planted his hands on his hips, pushing his suit coat out. "If things go bad, this is on you, not me."

"Let's get this party started," Logan said.

"Ready, hon?" Nick tugged at her arm.

"I'm not your hon," she said.

"I think that hickey says you are." Dylan slapped her shoulder as he breezed by.

"Welcome to the family," Logan said with a smile.

"You people are really weird," she muttered before turning her attention to Nick, who stood beside her with his arm still looped over her shoulders. "Next time I'm going to cover your neck in hickeys and see how you like it."

"Is that a promise?" He winked.

She jabbed his gut. "Let's go, *hon*, we've got work to do."

6

*N*ick leaned against the tractor trailer parked in the back lot behind Ramos' restoration and refurbishing warehouse, which is just one of the many businesses Ramos used to legitimize himself. More than half of the parking lot lights had burned out. Nick folded his arms across his chest, scanning the area, mentally picturing the exact location of every man he and his brothers had assembled.

They were the elite of the elite and capable of the impossible.

But if this was a set up, then Ramos would be expecting a raid.

"If this is what he uses as the Holding Tank, the outside perimeter isn't very secure with one night guard at the gate and the few on the roof." Logan sat on the wheel hood. Of all the Sarich boys, he'd been the most even-keeled, which made him the most like their father. His passing had affected all of them deeply, but

Logan took on the role of protector of his little brothers. Even though Nick had been essentially an adult when his father died, and Logan less than two years older than him, Logan had been the one that held the family together.

He still did.

"I've detected four cameras so far on the outside."

"Mia's working on hacking into Ramos' system to see what she can find out and get Dylan eyes on the inside, but since we don't have wires, we have no idea where we stand on that, and she's not answering my text."

"She'll let you know when she cracks it. Now we just need Ramos to show up." Based on what he'd learned about Ramos and his operation, Nick didn't feel confident that Ramos believed Nick and Leandra to be exactly who they pretended to be, which meant this plan wouldn't go off without a hitch.

Though, Nick had never had an op go completely as planned.

The sound of the truck door closing echoed across the night sky.

Nick turned his head to see Leandra stepping onto the running boards before letting her feet hit the pavement.

"He's late," she said as she stood with her hands on her hips, looking at the building.

"He's probably watching us." Nick reached out, grabbing hold of her biceps, and pulled her to his chest. "My only concern right now is if he had more armed security in places we didn't know about." He looped his arms around her sexy waist, letting his hand glide across the top of her ass.

"I'm sure Dylan's got it covered," Logan said.

"What are you doing?" she whispered, pressing her hands against his chest.

"Acting like a married couple." He tilted his head, leaning in for a kiss.

"We're not married. We're not anything." Her words might have indicated he should back off, but her body leaned against his as her fingers gently massaged his shoulders. Her tongue darted out of her mouth and licked her plump lips.

"Just killing time until Ramos shows his ugly face." He sucked her bottom lip into his mouth before slipping his tongue between her lips, twirling it against hers in a slow dance that ignited a flame deep in his gut. A fierce wave of protectiveness rolled over him like a hurricane slamming into the coast. He pulled back, taking in a deep breath, then letting it out slowly as he got lost in her dark, smoldering eyes. "Stay close to me no matter what happens."

She held his gaze for a long moment. "I'm a big girl. I can handle this."

"That's not the point." Other than his brothers, she was the only person he wanted covering his back. "We need to protect each other in the event this turns into a shitstorm."

She smiled.

And in that moment, he knew without a doubt,

she'd captured his heart, and he was never getting it back.

"We've got company," Logan said.

Nick kissed her sweet lips with a loud smack before lacing his fingers through hers, turning to face a black sedan rolling to a stop ten feet in front of them.

Ramos stepped from the back seat, leaving the door open, standing behind it. "You'll need to pull the rig to the loading dock."

"I'll do that," Logan said.

"Who the fuck are you?" Ramos scowled.

"I'm the guy with a million dollars…in cash," Logan shot back as he pulled open the tractor trailer door. "And if I really like what I see, I've got another two hundred thousand as a down payment for another shipment in a month."

"Thought you said you had two buyers?" Ramos said, his tone laced with frustration.

"I bought the other buyer out," Logan said.

"So, you're going to resell on the open market as an auctioneer?" Ramos rested his arm over the car door as he looked around.

Logan laughed. "I've got overseas buyers lined up, and like I said, I'll give you cash up front to get me more, if my customers and I are satisfied."

"Fair enough. But I want to see the money before you load anyone in your truck." Ramos waved his hand. "You two ride with me."

Nick nodded, tugging at Leandra's hand.

"Looks like the little lady might have delivered on her promise," Ramos said, smacking his lips.

"Not might have delivered. I did deliver," Leandra said as she slipped into the back seat of Ramos' vehicle. "And you owe us the rest of our finder's fee."

Nick fisted his hands as Leandra ended up between him and Ramos.

"What's your cut on the other end of this sale?" Ramos asked, daring to pat Leandra's leg.

"Keep your—" Nick started, but Leandra cut him off.

"What, if any, business we have with Logan is none of your concern. We hooked you up with someone who could move your merchandise now, someone you can do long-term business with, *and* you're getting paid a hefty sum of money."

When she rested her hand on Ramos' thigh, it took enormous control for Nick not to reach across the seat and strangle Ramos. Nick could picture the man's face turning bright red while Nick's fingers closed off Ramos' throat.

She leaned closer to Ramos. "If you ever touch me again." She slid her hand higher, closer to his groin. "I'll take you by the nuts and twist them so hard you will need surgery to put them back in the right place, only my husband will kill you before anyone has the chance to take you to the hospital."

Nick relaxed his fingers, biting back a smile, watching Ramos squirm in his seat. She must have some grip on his leg a little too close to where it counts.

"Is that so?" Ramos said with a shaky voice.

"We're not the kind of people you want to fuck with." She removed her hand and leaned against Nick. "Our contacts are far and wide, and we can have you taken out like that." She snapped her fingers.

"Guess we know who wears the pants in your family," Ramos said under his breath as the driver put the car in gear, easing toward the loading dock.

"I wouldn't have it any other way," Nick said, pride swelling in his gut.

The revving of the diesel engine roared across the quiet night. Nick scanned the building and surrounding area. He knew the exact location of each of the team members, but he couldn't see them. What he didn't know was if Fielding was actually going to follow the plan and wait until he got word from Dylan before charging in.

If he didn't, that would be bad on two counts.

First, if there were hostages in the building, it would put them at risk. Ramos wasn't necessarily the brightest criminal, but he wasn't stupid and probably had the holding area booby-trapped.

Second, if the hostages had been moved and Fielding and his agents charged, not only could the sky light up from gunfire, but he risked losing the trafficking charge, which brought with it a dozen other felony charges, potentially putting Ramos away for life.

Whereas the casino charge Ramos could possibly

fight, getting the charge and sentence reduced, not really shutting him down.

"How long has this group been held here?" Leandra asked.

"The longest resident would be two weeks. As I told you, there are fifty in all, ranging in age from twelve to twenty. The majority being females," Ramos said as the car rolled to a stop in front of a set of steel doors next to the loading dock.

Nick stepped from the car. His lungs stung from the scent of gas coming from the semi his brother backed up to the loading bay. The tractor trailer beeped in a continuous pattern until the truck screeched to a halt and Logan jumped from the cab.

"Where's the money?" Ramos barked.

The metal doors to the building rattled, and two heavily armed men stepped outside, followed by Alicia, who made eye contact but quickly turned away.

The jury was out on what side of the Ho Chi Minh Trail she sat on.

"Here is half." Logan tossed a bag, which landed with a thud about five feet from the truck. "You'll get the rest when everyone is loaded."

"I want to see the rest of it," Ramos said, a response that didn't surprise Nick in the least.

Logan turned on his heels, climbed back up in the cab, and pulled down another bag. "You want to look at it, you've got to come here."

"Alicia, get the cash and check out the rest," Ramos said with a clipped tone. "Let's settle our business. My men created a diversion for Agent Fielding, but we've only got thirty minutes before he's got eyes back on this building."

Nick's heart skipped a beat as he stared directly at Alicia who looked everywhere but at him.

Fielding had been adamant that his men had been undetected, but at this point, Nick figured that was only if Alicia was still one of the good guys. "How many eyes? And where have they been planted?" Nick asked, looking around again. Four office buildings stood several stories higher than the warehouse to the east. It would be easy for anyone on the top floor to keep an eye on the other side of the warehouse. To the west was the highway, but Fielding could have put a man up on one of the ramps. North and south were a little more complicated, but there were enough small businesses that could house a stakeout.

"A food truck across from Pendleton Offices and a tow truck from a garage down the other side of the street," Ramos said.

"What's the diversion?" Nick asked. Those had been the two stakeouts Fielding had copped to, but Nick suspected Fielding held back some intel. Damn Feds. Of all the organizations he'd worked with over the years, they'd been the least cooperative.

"It's covered; that's all you need to know." Ramos pointed toward Logan. "Open your loading doors and my guys will hook you up to the dock." Ramos waved them toward the front door. "Pardon the pat down, but if you're carrying, we're going to take your weapon. You can have it on the way out."

"No need." Nick handed over his Smith and Wesson as did his brother.

Leandra bent over, lifting up her pant leg and pulling her small handgun from its belt.

"Alrighty then." Ramos held his hand out in front. "Welcome to the Holding Tank."

Nick held Leandra's hand, probably a little too hard based on her sideways glance. While he had more power and strength, she definitely outsmarted him in most areas…except tactical, which was her only weakness, and if this plan went south, she, unfortunately, was their weakest link.

They followed the armed men through a short corridor and then into the main storage area.

"Isn't Alicia coming with us?" Leandra asked.

"She's going to count the money," Ramos said.

Nick strained to focus on the building. The only lighting provided was by a couple of flashlights. Various desks, sofas, and other home décor were set up in work stations. Ramos had built a reputation for being the king of restoration and was used by many of the rich and famous to make what was old, new again, creating unique pieces from any period of time.

No way did Ramos know anything about this business.

Just a front.

Nick noted the staircase at the far end of the building.

According to the blueprints, the second floor was where all the offices were located. He also noticed how new the inside of the building looked even though there hadn't been any permits or changes recorded by the county.

Which meant the plans they were working off were most likely wrong.

Ramos led them to a locked door in the corner of the west end of the warehouse. The room looked to be about twenty feet by thirty feet.

"Where is the merchandise?" Logan asked with short growl.

Nick understood the sentiment as he didn't want to step into what appeared to be a room with only one way out.

"Below us." Once the door clicked closed behind the group, Ramos flicked on an overhead florescent light. "When I took this warehouse over, I spent a little over a year adding a lower level. I originally used it for my casinos." Ramos stepped past a small desk and a couple of chairs, the only things in the room, to what appeared to be a closet, only behind the metal door was an old-fashioned warehouse elevator, complete with a metal cage.

Leandra squeezed his hand as she glanced at him with pursed lips.

The hair on the back of Nick's neck stood straight up.

They had all agreed that everything seemed too easy, but Ramos was under fire, and he knew Fielding had enough to arrest him.

But if Alicia had flipped? Fielding had jack shit, except whatever bad intel she gave him.

Ramos picked up a walkie-talkie from the desk. "Sending them down."

"We're ready for them," a voice crackled.

"You three go on down. I'll meet you outside." Ramos stepped back as his goons stepped forward, guns drawn.

"What the fuck is going on?" Leandra asked.

Nick tugged at her hand, but she didn't budge.

"Nothing's going on." Ramos held his hands up. "Merchandise is below. My men will guide you to the loading area. We'll complete our business outside."

Nick knew Ramos was full of shit, but what were his choices? Get shot here or down below? He figured the couple minutes in the elevator would be enough time to devise a plan.

Logan must have thought the same thing as he slowly backed up.

Ramos slid the door closed with a shitty grin.

"Motherfucker," Nick whispered, glancing around quickly. All four sides were lined with a metal grate, with only three concrete walls and one steel door that made it impossible to see out. However, he could see the shaft above, which indicated the elevator went up to the top floor as well.

"Ambush," Logan said.

"I bet they are going to use our truck to get the hostages out and drive right by Fielding, thinking it's us." Nick sucked in a deep breath.

"Probably the plan," Logan said, holding up a set of keys. "Though it might be hard for them to get anywhere without these."

A small piece of hope, but that was all they needed.

Nick shoved Leandra behind him while he stepped in front of Logan.

"What the fuck are you doing?" Logan punched his shoulder. "You're not a human shield."

"Back the fuck up. You've got a kid on the way and you're"—he pointed to Leandra—"well, my mother would kill me if I didn't try to protect you."

"Except you'll already be dead by the time she gets the chance." Leandra stepped to his side.

The motor kicked in, and the elevator rattled.

Logan lifted his pant leg and pulled out a couple handguns. "Here. Hopefully we're not too outgunned."

"Sorry, hon, but my brother and I are highly trained professionals, so please step behind me again," Nick said.

"Right, because I've never fired a damn weapon before." She laughed and bent over. "Are you the only asshole who didn't think to pack a second weapon?" She held up a pistol. "Not as impressive as your Smith and Wesson, but it will do the trick."

"I'm not an asshole," Nick muttered, retrieving both his spare weapons. "When you run out of ammo, you better be standing behind me."

"If you run out first, you get behind me." She cocked her head with her lips pursed. "Got it, *hon*."

Nick resisted the urge to kiss them until they were

bruised, but only because they didn't have time. If they survived this, he'd be putting hickeys all over her body.

Logan laughed. "You two are made for each other."

The elevator came to a halt, and the motor shut down. Nick held his weapons out and swallowed. This wasn't his first ambush. Hopefully it wouldn't be his last.

He took a few steps to the side. "Open the door but stay behind it."

Leandra nodded. Curling her fingers around the handle, she pulled back.

Nothing happened.

A loud thud from above echoed in the elevator. Nick looked up, and directly overhead was a green, oval object.

"Grenade," he said.

Without being asked, Leandra stepped away from the door, taking Logan's weapons as he yanked down on the lever, moving the door only slightly, but leaving enough room for Nick to curl his fingers around the edge, heaving it open.

"Move," he shouted as he grabbed Leandra and leapt from the elevator.

Bam!

The deafening explosion rang in Nick's ears as his body catapulted across the corridor. He held Leandra tight, covering her body with his as pieces of metal blew by. His back slammed against a wall so hard it rattled his teeth.

He groaned, feeling his skin tear.

"Hon?" He cupped Leandra's face, lifting her head. "Leandra?" His voice was muffled from the ringing in his head.

Her eyelids fluttered. "That was not fun."

He let out a soft chuckle, running his hands up and down her body, checking for possible injuries.

"Logan?" he called. A trickle of fear filled Nick's gut. Logan had been the last one out of the elevator shaft. "Logan?" he called louder, pushing himself to a standing position, pain ripping through his lower back.

He helped Leandra to her feet. "Anything hurt?"

"My head," she muttered, rubbing her temples. "Both my knees hurt, but since I'm standing, it's probably nothing too bad."

"Okay." Nick kissed her cheek. "I need to find my brother."

"I'm right here," Logan said, coming into view, holding his shoulder which looked as though someone had yanked it out of its socket. "Thank God for the long delay on that grenade." Blood ran down his arm.

"You're bleeding," Nick said.

"In a few places, but nothing that's gonna require stitches, like your back."

Nick twisted, lifting his shirt. "Fuck," he muttered.

"That looks nasty," Leandra said as she gathered up some of her shirt, wiping the blood away. "We need to stop the bleeding."

"We need to get the fuck out of here." Nick tore off his shirt, ripping it apart and tying it around his body, covering the wound.

"Before that, someone needs to put my mother-fucking shoulder back in its proper place," Logan ground out.

"I haven't done this in years." Nick pressed his hand on the back of Logan's shoulder, reaching around with the other. "You ready?" He didn't wait for an answer as he slammed Logan's shoulder.

"Fuuuucccck...you asshole." Logan grabbed his shoulder and rubbed vigorously before rotating it a few times.

"You're welcome. Now let's call in the cavalry."

"My phone is broken." Logan held up the shattered object. "How about yours?"

Nick pulled out his phone and stared at it. "Works, but no service."

Leandra held her phone up, moving it around before shoving it in her back pocket. "Mine too." She pressed one hand on his stomach, the other over the wound on his back, applying pressure.

Logan stood in front of the blown-out elevator door. "We can climb up, no problem."

"Not before we take a look around. Maybe the hostages are still here. At the very least, maybe we can find some records that will help me find my client's daughter," Leandra said.

Nick exchanged a long glance with Logan. "Dylan had to have seen or heard the blast."

Logan nodded.

Nick took Leandra by the shoulders. "We have to stick together, and if things get dicey again, we're out of here, okay, hon?"

She rolled her eyes. "Do you call the guys you work with in the field, hon?"

"Of course not." He laughed, tracing the mark he'd left on her neck. "And I don't give them hickeys either."

Yep. It was official.

He'd lost his ever lovin' mind.

7

*L*eandra's head felt like the grenade went off inside it, not in the elevator. Her knees stung from the scrapes that had ripped her flesh as she and Nick slid across the floor, slashing open her jeans.

Her entire body ached.

But not as much as her heart did.

A thud on the ceiling caught her attention. "Please, no more grenades."

Another thud.

Then three more.

"We've got company," Nick said before whistling three times.

Whoever was above them whistled back.

"Baby Dyl to the rescue," Nick said, pointing to a door at the end of the corridor. "Let's check that out."

She let out a long sigh of relief as she made her way down the hallway. She stood behind Nick, since he pushed his arm out and tucked her back there, while Logan opened the door and did a quick scan before giving them the 'all clear.'

Stepping into the room, her eyes immediately focused on the prison-like cells that occupied the room.

She gasped, sucking in air that tasted like three-day-old piss left in an unflushed toilet.

Coughing, she took a few steps forward, reaching out to one of the cells, letting her fingers glide across the cold metal bars. Tears stung the corner of her eyes. Bare cots lay on the cold tiled floor, a single dirty, thin blanket in each cell.

That was it.

"We have to find them," she whispered as she counted the cells.

Thirty-two.

A powerful arm skimmed across her lower back. The strength it offered rolled into her skin, entering her bloodstream, racing to her heart.

She sucked in as much of that strength as she could.

"Ramos couldn't have moved them far." Nick pulled her against his body. "We'll find them."

She turned her head. "And Skyler. Or at the very least, find out what happened to her. Her family needs closure no matter the outcome."

Nick nodded.

The door behind them rattled. Instinctively, she gripped her weapon, pulling it from the back of her pants and aimed it.

Three whistles.

Nick grabbed her wrist, lowering her arms. "That's my brother and his team."

The door opened, and Dylan and five other men, all dressed in dark clothing, all carrying rifles, strolled through the door as if they owned the place.

"Glad to see you're still standing," Dylan said with a smile. "Heard the blast and felt it, too."

"What took you so long to get here?" Nick said with a sarcastic tone.

"Ran into Ramos and his goons loading the hostages into the rig and thought we should deal with that before finding out if he'd successfully blown up your ugly asses." Dylan turned his attention toward Leandra. "And by that, I certainly don't mean yours, because your ass isn't ugly at all."

"Don't be commenting on her ass, or I'll have to beat the crap out of you," Nick said.

She rolled her eyes, then reached out and grabbed the fabric around Nick's waist and tugged.

He groaned.

She pointed to Dylan. "And my ass is out of your league."

Dylan's expression turned serious. "Ramos is in custody, and all the hostages are safe. We're going to transport them to a private hospital for medical attention and contact all their families."

"Thank you." She glanced around the room again. "I want to talk to Ramos." Her fingers itched to curl around his nuts and twist so hard they snapped.

"I doubt Fielding will let you," Dylan said, stepping to the side, giving her access to the door. "But I'd love to see you in action."

"Back the fuck up little brother," Nick said, taking three large steps.

"What did I tell you?" Logan laughed.

"He's so far gone, it's pathetic," Dylan said.

"Motherfuckers," Nick said under his breath.

Leandra opened her mouth to yell at all the brothers, but nothing came out. She cleared her throat. "I'm going to go talk to Ramos. You all are going to find me a paper trail that helps us find the others that Ramos has sold into a living hell." She pointed at each one of them. "Got it?"

"Yes, ma'am," Logan and Dylan said in unison.

"I'm going with you," Nick said.

She glared at him with her best scowl.

He pointed to his side, blood trickling from the soaked fabric. "I'm gonna bleed out if I don't find something to cauterize this hole or stitch it up."

"Fine." She noted the sweat beading on his forehead. "You can come with me," she said, trying to keep her tone more frustrated than concerned. She didn't want him or his damn brothers thinking she cared that much. "Put pressure on that wound, please."

"I've got a military grade first aid kit in the van," Dylan said.

"Good to know." She nodded.

They made their way back up the blown elevator shaft in silence. Once on the main floor, she looked down at the gaping hole and all the rubble. The reality of how close she'd come to death hit her senses like gale-force winds.

But the idea she could have lost Nick twisted her emotions so tight in her gut, it felt like a tornado had touched down and all her insides were about to be tossed outside.

She glanced at Nick. His skin had taken on a white-gray tone.

"Come on." She wrapped her arms around his middle, putting more pressure, feeling the tacky blood stick to her fingers. "Let's get you stitched up."

He leaned against her, his arm draped over her shoulders. "I'm sorry about the hon, thing. I'll be more conscious of it in the future."

"What future?" She hadn't meant to say that out loud, but now that it was out there, she might as well deal with it. Her heartbeat slowed as she wondered what it would be like to walk away from Nick Sarich the moment she completed her job. The thought felt like fingers reaching into her chest and squeezing her heart until it stopped beating altogether. "We both know whatever this is, it isn't real."

"I almost wish that were true." His lips pressed against her temple with the gentle touch of a feather. "For the first time in years, I find myself wanting to be with someone more than once or twice, and I'm not just talking about mind-blowing sex."

"I don't want to want somebody." She glanced in his direction, catching his gaze. "Not even you."

"I know," he said, pushing open the door with his hip. At least ten FBI vehicles had positioned themselves around the tractor trailer. Dozens of agents wearing FBI jackets filled the parking lot. "I understand."

"Thank you, for everything." Lame response, but it was all she had at the moment.

"Save your thanks for when we find Skyler." He groaned as he pointed toward a grouping of agents around one particular vehicle. "Let's talk to Ramos, then find that first aid kit."

"Other way around," she said.

"No. If we don't do it now, we might lose our opportunity. I'm not going to drop dead in the next fifteen minutes."

She took his hand and pushed it hard against his side. "Keep the pressure on, okay?"

"Will do." He leaned up against a car not far from where Fielding stood over Ramos, who had been handcuffed and sat in the back of one of the SUVs.

Alicia wasn't too far away, also handcuffed.

Leandra had never met anyone like Nick before. He was a complicated man, with so many different aspects to his personality. Loyal to the bone. Passionate about helping others. Fiercely protective of those he cared about.

And he did care about her.

Lying to herself about her own feelings toward him had become impossible.

But those feelings were connected to a shared loss.

A commonality so deep, it bound them together in a way no one else could understand.

At least she knew they'd walk away friends.

"Go get the information we need," he said.

A rush of adrenaline tickled her fingertips, building speed across her body like a raging river. She turned toward Ramos, but out of the corner of her eye, she saw Logan and Dylan moving quickly across the parking lot, waving her over.

She patted Nick on the chest before meeting his brothers halfway.

"What's up?" she asked, planting her hands on her hips, glancing over her shoulder at Ramos, who had the audacity to smile.

"We found something." Logan handed her a file. "Certain types of girls seemed to have been flagged for one specific buyer."

"Girl's like Skyler."

Logan nodded. "In the file are pictures of all the girls. Sixteen girls to be exact."

"Do we have the buyer's name?" she asked.

"Just a code name." Dylan tapped the file. "Hollywood."

She swallowed. "That could mean the buyer is in Hollywood or looks like a Hollywood type."

"There are other files, categorizing the hostages, so we'll need Fielding to get his team down there," Logan said.

"Thanks." She turned on her heels and marched

over to where Fielding stood, just a few feet from Ramos.

Fielding held up his hand. "Oh, no, you don't."

"Oh, yes, I do." She took one step past Fielding before he grabbed her arm. "Let go of me," she said in a dark tone behind gritted teeth.

"You're not going near him."

"I need to ask him about this." She shoved the file at Fielding. "The girl I was hired to find is in that file. I need to know who the buyer is."

Fielding stepped closer, encroaching on her personal space. "You're a low-life PI, and you have no authority to talk with anyone at this crime scene, and unless you want me to slap a set of handcuffs on you—"

"You'll do no such thing," Nick's voice boomed across the night sky. He stood between his two brothers, who helped him stand. "You're going to give her five minutes to find out what she wants, and then we're going to deliver that buyer to you on a silver platter, along with credit for this takedown."

She wanted to slap Nick for jumping in when she was perfectly capable of handling this situation, only it felt too damn nice to know someone had her back. She knew he hadn't stepped up because he didn't think she could handle it.

No. She knew him well enough to understand he only jumped in because he knew something she didn't.

"I'll handle my own interrogation," Fielding said, puffing out his chest.

"Don't make me sic my boss on you again," Dylan

said with a smile, holding up a military grade phone. "Shall I call him?"

Fielding narrowed his eyes. "Five minutes," he said with a snarl.

Whatever Dylan did for the United States Army, it had to be damn important.

Leandra didn't waste a second as she bolted toward Ramos.

"I'm going to fucking kill you." He stood, but the guard pushed him back down.

Her heart pounded so fast it hurt. Staring into the eyes of a man she knew for sure would kill her, if given the chance, made her pause for a moment. She'd gotten herself in some pretty crazy-ass situations, but this by far had been the most dangerous.

"Who is Hollywood?"

"You think I'm going to tell you that?" Ramos laughed, leaning in. "Better watch your back, sweetheart, because I'm coming for you."

She swallowed. "Where does Hollywood take the girls?"

Ramos shook his head. "You and your husband, or whoever the fuck he is, aren't going to live to see daybreak, much less find out anything about Hollywood."

Ramos was never going to tell her anything. She clenched her fist. "You're a piece of shit." She bent down, leaning so close to him she could feel his breath on her skin. She reached between his legs, gripping his testicles with all her might, and twisted.

He cried out like a cow being castrated.

"If anything happens to me, my *husband* is going to reach down your throat and grab your nuts." She squeezed harder. "And pull them out through your mouth."

She let go and spun around, making a beeline for Nick.

"Feel better?" Nick asked as she moved between him and one of his brothers, putting her arm around his waist and applying pressure to his wound again.

Nick groaned.

"I feel fucking fantastic." She tugged him across the parking lot, following one of his brothers toward a van. "But we have no idea who Hollywood is."

"Actually, we have a tip."

She glanced up at him, staring into his warm blue eyes. "Logan took pictures of the files and sent them to his fiancée who worked her computer geek genius and got us a lead."

"Then come on, Batman, let's get you fixed up and ready to roll."

"Whatever you say, Cat Woman."

"Rrrrroahhh." She laughed, shaking her head. "I have no idea how I'm going to repay you."

"I can think of a few ways."

---

8

*N*ick lay on his stomach on a mattress inside the small hangar of a private airport outside of Orlando while a cocktail of fluids, vitamins, and other nutrients were pumped into his veins.

"This is going to hurt," Leandra said as she pinched his skin. "Ready?"

"Go for it." He rested his forehead on the back of his hand, closing his eyes tight, letting out a slight groan as the thick needle pierced his skin.

Thankfully, Leandra ignored the noise and worked quickly, pulling his torn skin together. It wasn't the first time he'd been stitched up in the field, and it probably wouldn't be the last.

But it would be the last time Leandra mended his broken body.

Unfortunately, she'd pieced together his shattered heart, and that was going to hurt like hell when they went their separate ways.

Something wet ran over his skin, then burned.

He growled.

"Sorry," she whispered. "Just cleaning it up so it doesn't get infected." She placed the gauze over the cut. "All done."

He rolled to his side, pushing himself to an upright position, leaning against the wall. "Help me with this?" He pointed to the IV in his arm.

She nodded, pressing a piece of cotton over the needle and pulling it out. "Never thought I'd be doing this when I became a PI."

"You're a natural."

"I wouldn't go that far." She scooted sideways, putting her foot under her ass. "You and your brothers are something special."

"Just average men doing their jobs."

"Nothing average about you."

Her smile brought his warm blood to a boil in seconds. He stretched his leg out, resting it in her lap. "Next to most of the men and women I work with, I am."

"Humble, too." She shook her head. "Can I ask you something?"

"Sure."

"Why'd you join the Army?"

"After my wife died, I needed out of Jupiter, Florida. I think I would have lost my mind if I had stayed."

"I understand that, but you could have stayed a police officer by transferring to another city or even state."

He fluffed up a pillow and patted it, thankful that she moved next to him with her shoulder leaning against his. "Two reasons, really. One was I saw what it did for Logan after he'd lost his scholarship and the chance to play major league baseball. It gave him purpose."

"What's the second reason?"

He let out a long breath. "The adrenaline rush you get when you stare death in the eye."

"That's quite the experience." Her laugh filled the room and tickled across his bare skin.

He laced his fingers through hers. "But when you survive, you're still left with the pain of life."

She nodded.

He stared down at their hands, running his thumb over her cut up skin. Working with his brothers didn't happen very often, but he couldn't think of anyone else he'd want by his side in battle.

"You okay?"

"Just tired," he admitted, closing his eyes. "Ramey won't be here for another half hour, so we might as well rest a bit." He slid down, pulling her with him and tucking her ass up against him. With his arms looped around her, he allowed himself to relax. "You're the one who is special," he whispered before nibbling on her ear. "And irresistible."

She rolled in his arms, locking gazes with him.

The world around him blurred out in a dizzy haze of gray and black, bringing her porcelain-like skin and rosy, full lips into a technicolor kaleidoscope.

"What are we doing?" she asked, her eyes searching his for something he wasn't sure he had the answer to.

"Waiting to fly to Miami and find this Hollywood guy and bring Skyler home."

She pursed her lips, cocking her head.

He took her hand, kissing the soft skin in the swell of her palm before pressing it against her chest, looking for her heartbeat. "Pretending just a little that we don't hurt so bad that we'd almost rather stare death in the eye than live again." Two weeks ago, this sentiment would have been fact. For ten years, living had scared him more than dying. The only reason he didn't toss himself into the death wish pit had been his family.

His mother and all of his brothers had been his lifeline. They'd been there for each other through thick and thin. They'd all lain down their lives for each other.

Nick would lay down his for Leandra and not think twice about it.

"I know when this is over, you're going back to your PI office in New York, and I'll be heading back to Tampa and my next assignment." He fanned his thumb across her bruised cheek. He suspected the blast had caused a few more bumps and bruises on her body, and he wanted to kiss them all. "I can be a selfish man, and I want to have you until I can't have you anymore."

She splayed her fingers across his chest; her touch sizzled his skin like rain dropping on hot pavement, causing steam to rise. "We've got a half hour?" The left corner of her mouth lifted slightly as she raised both brows.

"Maybe a little less now." He took her chin between his thumb and forefinger, tilting her head and parting her perky lips. "Just enough time to make you scream my name."

"Might be the other way around." Her hand danced down his stomach, fiddling with the button on his pants.

He groaned as the tear of his zipper echoed in his ears. Her warm hand covered him as he grew harder. His chest heaved, sucking in a deep breath, staring into her beautiful dark eyes, getting lost in her. His tugged at her shirt, pulling it out of her pants. "This needs to come off now."

She got to her knees, lifting the tight fabric over her head. Her full breasts bounced in her lacy bra. He reached up, finding the clasp, freeing her glorious mounds into his hands. He kneaded them before taking her tight nipple into his mouth.

Her hands caressed his scalp, her fingers gliding through his hair in gentle strokes. When he glanced up to see her staring down at him with loving eyes, he paused, letting her nipple fall out of his mouth. Rising to his knees, he cupped her ass, pressing his mouth against hers. His tongue parted her lips, finding hers and engaging it in a slow and tender dance.

Enjoying the slowness, he carefully removed the rest of her clothing, enjoying the soft curves of her body. He kissed her ankles and the soft spot behind her knees. He caressed her round breasts as his tongue glided across her stomach, her hips lifting off the bed, encouraging him to give a little attention to the spot that made her a woman.

He kissed her swollen nub, lapping slowly, getting drunk on her taste. All he could think about was entering her at the precise exquisite moment her climax rocked her body, squeezing him tight.

The hunger to hear her call his name tugged at his control. He'd do anything to please her. To make her feel like she was the most special and important person in the world.

Gliding a few fingers into her warm and ready body, he glanced up.

She'd arched her back, lifting her hips toward him, tossing her head from side to side. He tried desperately not to care beyond those feelings he'd had over the years for other women.

But she wasn't other women.

And he had real, hard and fast, feelings for her. The kind you couldn't deny without letting a little piece of you die.

"Look at me," he said with a tight voice.

She jerked her head up, fists clutching the sheets. Her mouth parted slightly with her dark hair messy and wild.

His lungs burned with every breath he took. His heart beat in one continuous thud in his chest as he lowered his head, determined to show just how much he cared for her, which was crazy since they'd only known each other a few days, and under less than ideal circumstances. Not to mention, sex wasn't the best way to show a woman you loved...

He paused his motions for a couple of seconds, swallowing his thoughts. Caring and love were two different things.

Caring about someone, you could get over.

Loving them?

Damn, he really loved her.

"What?" she questioned with a panty breath.

"I want to live again."

Her eyes went wide.

He bit back a smile as her smoldering gaze turned soft and warm and filled with a mutual understanding and respect.

He'd take that as a sign she felt the same way but wasn't ready to fully accept it. However, he wasn't going to let her walk off without a fight.

The way her soft moans filled his ears sent the room spinning. He loved that he could please her with a simple soft touch of his fingers and tongue, making her hips grind against him, rolling faster and faster.

Knowing she was on the verge of release he sucked down hard, curling his fingers inside, finding that spot that made her body purr with passion.

"Oh...Nick!"

Music to his ears, her words sent a shiver from his head to his curling toes. He needed to be inside her, now.

Positioning himself over her with his hands just

above her shoulders, he entered her slowly, biting down on his lip as she squeezed herself around the length of him, her stomach still quivering and jerking.

"Leandra," he let out in a long breathy moan as her legs wrapped around him, her heels digging into his ass, pushing him all the way in. He swelled inside her heat, matching her stroke for stroke as she thrashed wildly beneath him.

She reached up, cupping his face, and drew his lips to hers, drawing his tongue into her mouth.

He did his best to control the rhythm, hoping to make it last a little while longer, but he gave up the moment she moved her lips to his neck and sucked.

A guttural groan tickled his throat as he swelled inside and then exploded.

"Leandra." He enjoyed the way her name rolled from his lips as she continued to suck and nibble on his neck and her body rocked with passion.

They held each other tight for long moments while their bodies slowly stopped convulsing. Rising up on his elbows, he fanned her cheeks with his thumbs, dropping his forehead to hers, realizing there was no barrier between them.

"We forgot something," he whispered, squeezing his eyes closed.

"What's…oh…shit. No protection."

He felt her legs release the tight hold they had on him.

"I'm sorry." He rolled off her, pulling her head to his

chest. "My job requires me to be tested, so I know I'm clean."

"I haven't had sex in two years, so you don't have to worry about that."

"Yeah." He swallowed. "Not really what I'm worried about."

The sound of a single engine plane approaching made it apparent this discussion would have to take place at a different time.

"Hear that?" he asked.

"I do," she said, rolling to her side, propping herself up on elbow.

"I'm really sorry," he said, staring into her deep eyes.

"It's as much my fault as it is yours, but I think the timing is wrong to really worry."

Thoughts of what could be filled his mind in a way that they shouldn't. An image of her with a swollen belly, carrying life, crashed into his brain over and over.

Tears stung his eyes as a different picture filled his mind. He couldn't go through the loss of another child.

"Wrong timing or not, you could be pregnant."

"I know that wouldn't be something you wanted, so whatever happens, I'll take care of it." She kissed his chest.

"What do you mean take care of it?" He bolted upright, groaning as he felt one of his stitches rip his skin. "If you're pregnant, I should—"

She covered his mouth. "If I am, we'll talk, but we won't know for a while, and we have a bad guy to go catch and a young girl to return home to her family, okay?"

He nodded, though this conversation was far from over. Craning his neck, he twisted his body, glancing at the gauze pad with a blood stain the size of a quarter. He frowned.

He wanted her.

And he'd want their baby, if she were pregnant.

They dressed quickly, then grabbed their gear and made their way out of the private quarters of the hangar and onto the runway in silence.

"What the hell kind of plane is that?" Leandra asked as they approached a four-seater plane that didn't look like any other plane in the world with its long body, high wings, and aerodynamic shield that could only be designed by a man who could fly anything with wings and an engine.

Ramey stepped from the other side of the plane. "This is Roxi, and I designed and built her myself."

"You didn't have to come all the way from New Mexico for this." Nick opened his arms for a brotherly hug which resulted in a groan as Ramey hit his wound.

"Shit. Sorry, bro. Forgot you were injured." Ramey was known as the runt of the litter, topping out at just shy of six feet. "You must be the famous Leandra." Ramey held his arms out. "We hug it out in this family."

"Take your eyes and hands off her. See that mark?" Nick pointed to her neck. "That's mine, so back the fuck up little brother."

Ramey laughed, pulling Leandra in for a quick hug despite Nick's threatening tone.

"Have you seen the mark she left on *your* neck? Geez, Logan and Baby Dyl warned me the two of you were all hot and bothered."

"Oh, my God." Leandra said as she poked Ramey in the chest. "Can we get going now? I've got a job to do."

"Yes, ma'am," Ramey said. "Just got word that Logan and Dylan have eyes on the target."

"Good," Leandra said.

Nick tilted his head and watched as the hottest ass on the planet swayed with each step she took into the plane. He let out a long sigh.

"First Logan and Mia? Now you've gone and fallen head over heels for that one? This is really going to ruin my visit with Mom. She'll for sure now have a date lined up for me with what she thinks is the perfect woman, and I'll have to be all polite, but then when I never call the chick back, Mom will be tugging at my ear. Why'd you have to go fall in love?"

"Shut up." Nick snagged the headset, smiling. He had it bad, and he was going to find a way to make Leandra see they were meant for each other. "Someday some chick is going to flatline you."

9

The flight from Orlando to Miami left Leandra wanting to stick her head in a garbage can and heave. It seemed of all the Sarich brothers, Ramey had to be the biggest adrenaline junkie. While she was sure he was a capable pilot, he didn't need to prove it by showing her what his homemade plane built from spare parts in his New Mexico garage could do.

Now sitting in the back of a helicopter, with Ramey again at the controls, her stomach turned and twisted.

The words *I want to live again* churned in her brain.

She held her stomach. The idea she could be pregnant terrified her on so many levels. If she were, she knew she'd want it. Love it.

She glanced at Nick, who looked in the other direction. She'd lost a husband.

He lost a wife and a child.

Not that she was comparing their pains, but she

couldn't imagine what that could have been like. Regardless, the mere idea she was carrying his child warmed her body like a heated blanket on a cool winter night.

"Touch down in two minutes," Ramey's voice crackled over the headphones, snapping her thoughts to the present situation.

Nick undid his restraints and stood, flinging a duffel bag over his shoulder. "As soon as the chopper hits the sand, jump, keeping your head down." He made a swirling motion with his hand. "Once Ramey is back up in the air, we'll need to hightail it to the first checkpoint."

"We're sure Dylan is inside at the party?" How Dylan managed an invite to a private party at a criminal's house, she could only imagine.

"He's there," Nick said, tapping his headphones. She removed hers and then unfastened her harness, making her way across the cargo hold, grabbing one handhold to the next, hoping she wouldn't fall out.

The ocean roared to her right as the wind pushed the chopper inland. Only the moon and a few stars managed to break through the inky darkness.

She tried to swallow but couldn't. It was like something too big was lodged in her throat, preventing her from getting air. Her hands shook as she gripped the side of the chopper, the sand coming up to greet them like a twister.

Nick took her hand, and they jumped. The swooping of the helicopter blades filled the air, and the roar of the engine rattled her brain. A split second later, the chopper faded off in the distance as she ran with Nick across the beach and to the mansion owned by Brett "Hollywood" Donaldson, an ex-porn star turned producer.

Once at the back gate, they crouched down behind the bushes. The sound of music and laughter filled the air. She peered over Nick's shoulder as he pulled out his cell phone, tapping open a text from Dylan.

Nick held the cell up so she could read it too.

One guard at checkpoint. I'll take him out when you're here.

Nick quickly texted back.

Here.

She rested her hands on Nick's shoulders, holding her breath, staring at the phone. The wind howled, rustling the bushes. What sounded like a smack, grunt, and thud echoed with the sound of branches hitting the metal fence.

The gate swung open, the wind catching it, shoving it backward against a brick wall. It bounced a few times. Dylan appeared in a pair of blue shorts and a button-down pink shirt, looking like the poster boy for some preppy clothing store. Ten degrees cooler and he'd have a sweater draped over his shoulders with the sleeves tied at his chest.

"Welcome to the party," Dylan said.

Nick zipped open the duffel bag, tossing out a pair of high heels. "How's that gun feel up your skirt?"

"Not as good as yours?" she shot back without thinking that statement through.

"Keep saying stuff like that and I'll start calling you *hon* again." Nick smoothed down the front of his yellow button-down shirt sported over green shorts.

She looked him up and down.

"Like what you see?" Nick smiled.

"I'm impressed you can carry the style off," she said, slipping her feet into a pair of three-inch fuck-me heels. "I think this makes me exactly your height," she said.

"Would make it easy to hike up—"

"Let's go, lovebirds," Dylan interrupted his brother as he held the fence back. "Next rotation for guards is in two hours, so we've got some time."

"Who else is inside?" Nick asked as they strolled up the walkway, his hand resting on the small of her back. The simple protective gesture could be taken as though he cared for her.

"Logan is in a tree near the pool house. Ramey's got a drone above us," Dylan said.

She looked up but didn't see anything. "I need you guys for all my missing person's cases."

"We're always available to family," Dylan said, patting her shoulder.

"I'm not family," she said, ignoring the tingle the word 'family' sent through her bloodstream.

"Those matching hickeys might as well be wedding bands," Dylan said as they rounded a corner in the path that opened up into the pool area.

Nick adjusted his collar. "Focus on the mission, asshole," he muttered.

An eighties' rock anthem belted through an impressive sound system. Women in bathing suits made of more string than fabric walked around serving drinks.

They stood just outside the pool deck, still hidden in the trees. She scanned the area, becoming painfully aware of her size. Every woman she could see had to be a size six or less. It had taken her a long time to be comfortable in her own skin and even longer to believe and feel her body was beautiful. She ran her hand down her stomach. Her body had muscle, but it also had curves.

At least your body is proportionate. Imagine if you had no boobs, you'd look like a pear, or no ass. That would be a real shame. Her mother's words jostled around in her brain as some skinny chick whipped off her bathing suit top, and her oversized fake boobs didn't even bounce as she jumped into the pool.

Instinctively, Leandra grabbed her own breasts.

Nick laughed, his hand squeezing her hip as he pulled her close. "You're the sexiest woman in this place," he whispered, kissing her temple.

"Thank you." She smiled at him, knowing he meant what he said.

Dylan held up a small circular object. "Ramey and Logan will be able to hear everything, but we're flying blind, so to speak."

She nodded, letting Nick attach the listening device to her blouse, his fingers grazing the top of her breasts.

"When we find Skyler, or find her location, just say, 'I need another drink' and then meet down by the gate where we came in," Dylan said with his hands in his pockets as if he hadn't a care in the world but taking in the view of breasts bobbing on the surface of the water. "If at any time you feel as though you're in danger or need assistance of some kind, just say, 'I need the bathroom.' Ramey and Logan will find you."

"And how do we find out if someone else finds Skyler or that we need to leave? Can we use our cell phones?"

"Only as a last resort. They have a rule about pictures, and if they see a phone, they will take it and kick you out," Dylan said, raising his finger to his throat. "Only thing is I believe if that happens, you'll be leaving in a body bag."

Nick turned, slipping his hands around her waist. "We don't have to split up."

"We'll cover more ground if we do."

He tightened his lips. "I'd rather we didn't."

"I'm a big girl, and I know what I'm doing."

"Not in this type of op you don't," Nick said with an arched brow. "You're staying with me."

"No. I'm not."

"But what if…if…" He pressed his lips to her ear. "What if you're pregnant?"

"We had sex like five minutes ago. I think that might take a bit of time to develop." She shook her head. "How much time do we have again?"

"Ninety minutes until we meet back at the gate," Dylan said.

"Let's get this party started." Leandra didn't wait for either Sarich brother to say a word as she strolled down the path, away from the protection of the trees, and on to the pool patio.

She took a drink off a tray from one of the half-naked girls, who didn't look overly thrilled to be serving anyone anything.

The beach house, if you could call a twenty-thousand-square-foot building a house, was lit up like the Fourth of July with decorative lights everywhere. As she strolled by a table with a group of people snorting cocaine off some chick's ass, she watched people coming and going from the main house. She needed to get in there.

Out of the corner of her eye, she saw Nick strolling on the other side of the pool, his hands in his pockets, smiling to all the hot women who approached him.

Focus.

She continued toward the house, figuring she'd enter through the open sliders on the far-right side.

"Hey, babe, can I buy you a drink?" a man asked as he approached, smacking her ass.

She held her glass up. "I've got one, thanks."

"How about I get you something else?" He grabbed her ass, squeezing and shaking it.

"Don't think my husband would appreciate that." She nodded in Nick's direction as she peeled the slimy hand off her butt cheek.

"What kind of man brings his wife to a party like this?"

She smiled sweetly. "I brought him. Now, if you excuse me, I have some business to take care of."

The gun strapped to her thigh gave her a sense of comfort, but if she had to pull it out, that would be bad no matter how one looked at it.

She made her way into what appeared to be the living room. White leather sofas filled the center, and white end tables and lamps accented the space. White paintings and artwork lined the walls.

The white room.

A circular staircase, with white steps, was situated on the far-right side of the room. A few young women dressed in schoolgirl skirts and blouses tied beneath their breasts wobbled down the stairs.

Behind them, older men adjusted their pants as they laughed and smiled and told a few dirty jokes.

Dylan strolled across the room with a girl dressed in the same tiny outfit as the other girl on his arm.

Fuck.

Skyler.

He looked directly at Leandra but didn't nod or give her any kind of signal. It was like he looked right through her, but maybe that was the signal.

Skyler had her hair in pigtails and a washed-out look on her face.

"I'm following," she whispered, figuring someone knew that Dylan had the girl.

When she got to the bottom of the steps, she looked

around, hoping no one noticed her. She raced to the top just in time to see Dylan open a door down the hallway. A guard at the top of the stairs stopped her.

"She's with me," Dylan called.

The guard shrugged. "Whatever floats your boat."

Leandra scurried down the hallway, ducking into the room. Skyler sat on the bed, barely aware of her soundings.

"She's strung out," Dylan said as he closed and locked the door before making his way to the window.

"Skyler?" Leandra whispered, sitting on the bed next to her.

Skyler raised her hands to her top and started to untie her blouse.

Leandra placed her hand over Skyler's, who looked at her with a blank expression. "I've seen two other girls dressed like this." Leandra took a blanket and wrapped it around Skyler.

"I believe there are five girls total here." Dylan opened the window. "Logan, Ramey. Second floor. Last window on the east side. Single guard at the top of the stairs. Need someone to take him out and replace him, then someone else to go to the living room bar and buy up all the girls in schoolgirl outfits and bring them upstairs so we can extract them."

"How are we going to do that?" she asked.

"Cause a power outage and climb out this window."

"Sounds easy enough." She pulled out her phone. "I'm going to text Nick."

"Let's wait on that," Dylan said.

"Okay." She wrapped her arms around Skyler's trembling body. "There were sixteen girls on that list."

"I don't think they are all alive. Hollywood keeps these girls so doped up they don't know who they are half the time. He uses them for porno movies, as prostitutes for parties like these, and God knows what else."

Leandra shivered, running her hands up and down Skyler's arms.

"What do you want with me?" Skyler tried to undo her shirt again.

"Nothing, sweetheart. We're here to bring you home."

Leandra jerked when someone knocked at the door. She glanced over at Dylan, who raised his weapon.

"Fuck off, I'm busy," he yelled.

"Open the damn door," Nick's voice rang out.

Leandra jumped to her feet as her heart pounded out of her chest. As soon as she pulled open the door, she wanted to throw herself in his arms, but instead, she helped the two girls Nick had with him to the bed.

"What the fuck is this?" one girl slurred out. "I hate orgies."

The other girl flung herself at Nick, trying to grab him. "Not here for that." He took her by the shoulders and sat her on the bed. "We're here to get you out of this hellhole."

"Yeah, right, whatever," the girl said.

"That was fast," Dylan said.

"When I saw Logan wandering around trying to

145

look like he wanted to get laid by some random chick, I knew something was up."

"That's fucking hilarious," Dylan said.

"Where is Logan?" Leandra asked.

"He's guarding the stairs, waiting for the two men who bought time with the other girls. He'll tie them up in one of the other rooms and bring the girls here." Nick leaned against the wall. "Then we make the lights go out and get these girls home."

"You're really going to get us out of here?" the girl who seemed semiconscious asked.

"We are," Leandra said.

The girl buried her face in her hands and started to sob.

A drone appeared in the window at the same time as Logan pushed open the door, and two more girls entered the room.

"What the hell?" One of the girls stumbled, falling to the ground. She looked up with fear in her eyes. "What are you going to do with us?"

"They're going to take us home," the sobbing girl said.

"No shit?" the girl on the floor asked.

"We need to start moving," Dylan said, pointing out the window. "We've got reinforcements on the ground, so as soon as the lights go—"

The room went dark.

"Move, move, move," Nick commanded holding up a small light.

Leandra and Nick helped gather the girls at the

window. Logan and Dylan tossed them over their shoulders one by one and slid them down a pulley to a group of men waiting to take them to safety. They worked quietly and efficiently, and in a matter of five minutes, they had all the girls out of the room.

"Let's go, Leandra," Dylan called.

The roar of the power kicking back on rattled the room as the lights flickered and the music bleeped back.

Leandra turned to face Nick.

But he was gone.

Then the room went black again.

10

*N*ick twisted his wrists, the rope digging into his skin. He blinked his eyes open. The searing bright light sent his pounding headache into a full-on battle of the drums.

"You fucked with the wrong man." A dark raspy voice pierced through the ringing in Nick's ears.

Nick struggled to concentrate as a sticky liquid dripped over his eyes.

"I could say the same thing to you." Nick's vision slowly snapped into focus. He'd been tied to a chair, his arms behind his back, his ankles bound to the legs. To his right a large oak desk faced a window that overlooked a small patio that he recognized as an extension of the pool area.

So he was on the first floor, east of the pool, and a far distance to the gate where he'd entered the property.

He glanced to his left, and his heart dropped to his gut.

Leandra sat on the sofa, her hands and ankles bound and duct tape over her mouth.

"Motherfucker." He snapped his head up to his captor. "You hurt her, and I'll fucking kill you." He cocked his head. "On second thought, I'm going to kill you anyway."

The man laughed. "I don't think so." He waved his gun in Nick's face, then pointed it at Leandra. "You stole my girls, so I'm thinking I should steal yours."

Nick growled, twisting his wrists as hard as he could. The rope ripped at his skin, but he didn't care. "You have no idea who you're dealing with." He had to believe his brothers had gotten the girls to safety and were minutes away from crashing through a window. Or maybe a door. He looked up. Could be the roof.

But his brothers were out there, and they would help save his sorry ass.

Their father always told them that brothers shared a bond, one that could never be broken. He taught them to watch each other's back. His father had been the smartest man Nick had ever known, and he and his brothers did their best to think just like him. Two days before he'd been killed in the line of duty, he'd gathered his sons and took them on a fishing trip, where they caught absolutely nothing but were reminded of the brotherhood they shared.

One for all and all for one.

Just one of the many Sarich family mottos.

"What? I'm supposed to be scared of some hired mercenary? No one is coming for you. Whoever you work for will write you off because what you just did is just as illegal as my operation."

"Like I said, you have no idea who you're dealing with." Nick slowed his breathing, controlling his pulse, letting all his training kick in. He had to keep his emotions, his feelings, for Leandra out of his head, or they might not live to see his brothers' plan.

Whatever that might be.

"Hollywood, right? That's what you go by?"

Hollywood nodded as he sat down next to Leandra, his slimy fingers on her leg.

Nick twisted his wrists harder, the extra force allowing him to snag the end of the rope with the tips of his fingers. Leandra's eyes shifted from Hollywood, then back to Nick.

"I bet this one has a pussy that tastes like the finest wine money can buy." Hollywood ran his hand between her legs.

Leandra shifted her eyes again, but this time Nick realized she wasn't looking at Hollywood, but at the window.

He stole a glance and cracked a smile when he saw the drone in the distance.

His brothers were close.

"You're right about that," Nick said, still tugging and twisting the rope. "But you're never going to find out."

"I beg to differ." Hollywood palmed Leandra.

Nick had had about enough of another man

touching what was his. "Let me tell you how this is going to go down because in a few minutes, I won't be sitting in this chair, and my hands are going to be around your neck."

"Really? And how is that going to happen, exactly?" Hollywood grinned, leaning way too close to Leandra's breasts.

"Come over here and I'll tell you."

"Why would I do that when I can fondle this lovely slut all I want?" Hollywood grabbed her boob and squeezed.

Leandra narrowed her eyes, raising her bound arms, nailing him just under the chin with a loud smack.

His head jerked back as Leandra scooted down the sofa.

"Bitch." Hollywood stood, looking down at her. "You're going to be sorry you did that," he said with a raised hand.

"In less than two minutes, a team of highly trained professionals are going to come crashing through that door." Nick nodded toward the entrance near the window. He needed to get Hollywood closer.

Hollywood took five long strides across the room, pressing his gun to Nick's temple, leaning in inches from his face. "In the last twenty minutes, I've doubled my security and gotten rid of anyone who doesn't belong here."

Nick smiled. "No, you haven't." He smashed his forehead into Hollywood's nose.

Hollywood screamed, dropping the weapon and grabbing his bloody face.

Nick leaned forward, then flung himself backward, destroying the chair as he crashed against the floor.

The sound of shattering glass filtered through Nick's brain as he continued to work the rope around his wrists.

Seconds later, Dylan stood over him, cutting through the ropes that bound him. He twisted his head to see Ramey helping Leandra out of her constraints and Logan standing over Hollywood, a gun to his face.

Their father would be proud.

Their mother? Oy. He rubbed his ear, remembering how much it hurt when she'd tugged at it each time they did something she didn't approve of.

Which was often.

He took the hand Dylan offered and hoisted himself to a standing position before charging the piece of shit lying on the floor.

Shoving his brother to the side, he hoisted Hollywood up by the collar. Nick cocked his fist and swung. Blood spurted from Hollywood's cheek as Nick's knuckles connected to bone.

"That's for what you did to those girls, you sick piece of shit." Nick wrapped his fingers around Hollywood's neck. "This is for touching my girl."

"Nick," Logan yelled. "It's over."

Nick stared into Hollywood's wide eyes as the man struggled to breathe, his hands grasping Nick's forearm.

"Nick," Leandra said, her warm hand gliding across his skin. "Let him go."

He let out a long breath as he eased his grip, then released Hollywood. "I hope you rot in hell." Nick straightened his back.

Sirens rang out as the clank of combat boots echoed from down the hallway.

Nick stiffened, causing a wave of dizziness, and he stumbled, grabbing ahold of Leandra. "You okay?" he asked.

"I'm fine, but I'm not so sure about you." She pressed her hand on his back. "Besides reopening this wound, you've got a nasty gash to your head and one on your arm."

He looked down, noticing one of his brothers tying a tourniquet on his left biceps just below the shoulder. "Well, fuck."

"Let's get you patched up again," Dylan said, looping Nick's good arm around his shoulders.

"Hang on," Leandra said as she marched over to where Hollywood leaned up against the wall, holding his bloody nose.

"She's not going to do it, is she?" Dylan asked.

"I think she is." Nick smiled.

"Do what?" Ramey asked.

"I'd cover your ears if I were you, little brother." Nick knew it was so terribly wrong to let her, but damn, the man did violate her.

She bent over, reaching between Hollywood's legs.

He let out a high-pitched squeal.

"That's for grabbing me."

Hollywood screamed like a dying pig.

"And that's for making my man bleed."

She stood, turning on her heels, brushing her hands together as if she were washing away dirt. "We can go now."

"Remind me never to piss off your girlfriend," Ramey muttered.

Nick's heart swelled with a combination of pride and terror.

They still had unfinished business, and no way in hell was he letting her just walk out of his life.

Ever.

11

FOUR WEEKS LATER...

*N*ick propped his pillow up, staring at the waterfall of hair flowing over his chest, Leandra's arm draped over his bare stomach.

He glanced out the window of his brother's guest room. Custom built homes on acre lots lined along the palm-tree-dotted quiet Orlando street.

Logan living in the 'burbs, about to get married, and with a baby on the way.

Life and it's strange turn of events.

Leandra let out a soft purr as she stretched. "What time is it?"

"Almost nine." He brushed her hair from her face.

"Why'd you let me sleep so late?" Her eyelids fluttered.

"You need it." He smiled. "Ready to meet my mother?"

"No." She pulled the sheet over her head. "Can't it wait until your brother's wedding?"

"That's not for another month." Nick laughed. "Come on, it can't be worse than how I met your parents. I mean, really. Nice introduction." He tugged at the covers, tilting her chin. "Hey, Mom and Dad, this is Nick, and oh, by the way, I'm pregnant, and it's his."

She smiled. "I was just killing two birds with one stone. I don't know who looked more shocked. You or my dad. But really, it's not like you didn't know it was possible."

"So not the point." He brought his mouth to hers, pressing his tongue between her lips. After everything had gone down in Miami, he'd gone back to New York with her for a few days before he was sent on another assignment, which took a week. When he returned, she'd dropped the bomb, one he hoped she'd drop, but the idea he would be a father still rattled his nerves.

Especially when he'd yet to tell the baby's mother that he loved her.

"You're trembling," she whispered.

"My mother still scares me." But that wasn't what caused the fear swirling in his gut.

What if Leandra didn't love him back?

They hadn't talked of marriage or being together as a couple; although, every time they were together, they ended up in bed.

She could have stayed in one of the other guest rooms, but she didn't say no to staying with him.

Or meeting his mother.

"Wonderful. Now I'm even more terrified." Leandra

let out a long sigh. "What time is she supposed to be here?"

"She's already here."

"What!" Leandra bolted upright. Her tank top shoulder strap fell down her arm. His boxers rolled down low over her hips.

"She got in yesterday, but since we got in so late, she was already asleep. I'm sure she's down in the kitchen making food for everyone."

"We're eating brunch here?" Leandra slapped his arm. "You should have told me that. I thought I was meeting her at some public restaurant where she'd have to be nice to me."

"You're carrying her grandchild. She's going to love you."

"I wanted her to like me for me, not because you knocked me up."

"Well, same went for your folks, but you shoved me under the bus."

She leaned back in the bed, her shoulder rubbing against his. "That's different."

"I don't see how."

For a week now, he'd been trying to find the perfect moment to tell her he loved her and wanted to marry her, but every time a moment came, something like her parents, or his mother, ended up ruining that moment.

"What the fuck," he muttered.

"Excuse me?"

He jumped from the bed and rifled through his rucksack until he found the little box. With trembling fingers, he climbed back onto the bed, hiding the box behind his back.

"I've wanted to say this for a while now, but honestly, something gets in the way, or I'm just afraid." He sucked in a deep breath and let it out in a long swish before looking her in the eye.

She smiled sweetly, her brown eyes melting his heart like a marshmallow over a campfire.

"I love you." He braced himself for the 'oh, well, I don't feel the same way, just having fun, but we can co-parent' rejection.

"I love you, too." She cocked her head.

He blinked, shoving a finger in his ear, wondering if he still suffered from temporary hearing loss. "What?"

"Why are you acting so surprised? It's not like we haven't said that before."

He coughed. "We've never said those words. I'd remember since I've been terrified for weeks that you'd tell me all our future would be was occasional screwing and co-parenting."

"Oh, my God. We've never said we loved each other?"

He shook his head.

"But I've known for a while you love me. How could you not know? Don't I show it?"

He nodded. "Yeah, but I need the words."

"I love you," she said, cupping his face and smacking his lips. "Better?"

"I'd feel a lot better if you put this on your finger." He opened the box and held it out in front of her. It wasn't a huge diamond, because he knew her well enough to know she wouldn't want that.

"Nicholas Emmerson Sarich," his mother's voice yelled from somewhere a little too close.

The hair on the back of his neck stood at attention. Nothing terrified him more than when his mother used his full name.

"The door is locked, right?" Leandra asked, staring at him, while he still held the engagement ring in front of her.

The door rattled.

"I guess not," he said softly as the door flew open.

"Logan tells me Leandra is here…" His mother's words trailed off as she planted her hands on her hips, glaring at him.

"You didn't tell her I was coming?" Leandra asked.

Nick wanted to crawl under the bed. If he had told his mother, they wouldn't have had a second alone the moment he'd set foot in this house.

"No, dear, he didn't. I thought I was going to have to fly to New York to meet the woman strong enough to bring this one to his senses." His mother grabbed him by the ear and yanked.

"Mom, really?" Heat spread across his cheeks. "You're embarrassing me here."

"Well, maybe if you'd told me, I wouldn't have to come barging in." His mother let go of his ear and held out her hand. "I'm Catherine Sarich and the mother to this idiot. Nice to meet you."

"Nice to meet you too."

He watched Leandra and his mother shake hands right next to a ring he still held in his palm.

"Well, breakfast will be ready in fifteen minutes. Don't be late," his mother said, turning on her heels, but she stopped at the door and glanced over her shoulder. "I'm going to tell you two something similar to what I told Logan and Mia."

"Oh, God, Mother, please don't." He rubbed his ear.

"I know you've both been married before, and I'm never going to be mother of the bride, so do what you want about that. But do not make me wait too long for lots of Sarich grandbabies."

"You'll only have to wait about seven and a half months," Nick said with a smile, enjoying the way his mother's eyes widened with her mouth hanging open.

She let out a breath and shrugged. "Well, it's only fitting we have another shotgun wedding since that's how your father and I did it."

"What!?" That was news to Nick. "I'm shocked, Mother."

His mother laughed as she gently closed the door.

"Well, that was entertaining," Leandra said, taking the ring out of the small box and sliding it on her ring finger. "Embarrassing, but highly amusing." She reached out and snagged his ear.

"Ouch!"

"I'll have to thank your mother for showing me how to keep you in line for the next fifty years."

Nick batted her hand away. "Interesting way to say yes to a marriage proposal."

"I have a feeling our life together is going to be very interesting."

Thank you for taking the time to read *Her Last Hope.* Next up in the series is *The Last Flight,* which is Ramey Sarich's story! You can download it today!
Sign up for Jen's Newsletter (https://dl.bookfunnel.com/rg8mx9lchy) *where she often gives away free books before publication.*

Join Jen's private Facebook group (https://www.facebook.com/groups/191706547909047/) where she posts exclusive excerpts and discuss all things murder and love!

ABOUT THE AUTHOR

Welcome to my World! I'm a USA Today Bestseller of Romantic Suspense, Contemporary Romance, and Paranormal Romance.

I first started writing while carting my kids to one hockey rink after the other, averaging 170 games per year between 3 kids in 2 countries and 5 states. My first book, IN TWO WEEKS was originally published in 2007. In 2010 I helped form a publishing company (Cool Gus Publishing) with NY Times Bestselling Author Bob Mayer where I ran the technical side of the business through 2016.

I'm currently enjoying the next phase of my life...the empty NESTER! My husband and I spend our winters in Jupiter, Florida and our summers in Rochester, NY. We have three amazing children who have all gone off to carve out their places in the world, while I continue to craft stories that I hope will make you readers feel good and put a smile on your face.

Sign up for my Newsletter (https://dl.bookfunnel.com/ 6atcf7g1be) where I often give away free books before publication.

Join my private Facebook group (https://www.facebook.com/

groups/191706547909047/) where I post exclusive excerpts and discuss all things murder and love!

Never miss a new release. Follow me on Amazon:amazon.com/author/jentalty

And on Bookbub: bookbub.com/authors/jen-talty

NEON SASS

PAINTING SASS

Boxsets

LOVE CHRISTMAS, MOVIES

UNFORGETABLE PASSION

UNFORGETABLE CHARMERS

A NIGHT SHE'LL REMEMBER

SWEET AND SASSY IN THE SNOW

SWEET AND SASSY PRINCE CHARMING

PROTECT AND DESIRE

SWEET AND SASSY BABY LOVE

CHRISTMAS AT MISTLETOE LODGE

THE PLAYERS: OVERCOMING THE ODDS

CHRISTMAS SHORTS

CHRISTMAS DREAMS

Novellas

NIGHTSHADE

A CHRISTMAS GETAWAY

TAKING A RISK

WHISPERS

Made in the USA
Monee, IL
20 May 2025

17800576R00105